WHEN
YOU
OPEN
YOUR
EYES

WHEN YOU OPEN YOUR EYES

CELESTE CONWAY

Simon Pulse

NEW YORK   LONDON   TORONTO   SYDNEY   NEW DELHI

SIMON PULSE

An imprint of Simon & Schuster Children's Publishing Division
1230 Avenue of the Americas, New York, NY 10020
First Simon Pulse edition March 2012
For information about special discounts for bulk purchases,
please contact Simon & Schuster Special Sales at 1-866-506-1949
or business@simonandschuster.com.
The Simon & Schuster Speakers Bureau can bring authors to your live event. For more
information or to book an event contact the Simon & Schuster Speakers Bureau
at 1-866-248-3049 or visit our website at www.simonspeakers.com.
Designed by Bob Steimle
The text of this book was set in Edlund.
Manufactured in the United States of America
2 4 6 8 10 9 7 5 3 1
Library of Congress Cataloging-in-Publication Data
Conway, Celeste.
When you open your eyes / Celeste Conway. — 1st Simon Pulse ed.
p. cm.
Summary: In Buenos Aires, where her father is the legal attaché at the U.S. Embassy,
sixteen-year-old Tess falls in love and tries to live the fast and free life of her friends
until she discovers the devastating consequences of ignoring rules.
[1. Conduct of life—Fiction. 2. Self-perception—Fiction. 3. Family life—Argentina—Fiction.
4. Americans—Argentina—Fiction. 5. Diplomats—Fiction.
6. Buenos Aires (Argentina)—Fiction. 7. Argentina—Fiction.] I. Title.
PZ7.C7683Whe 2012
[Fic]—dc22
2011010341
ISBN 978-1-4424-4229-0 (hc)
ISBN 978-1-4424-3031-0 (pbk)
ISBN 978-1-4424-3032-7 (eBook)

To Colette and Veronica

THE
FIRST
PART

I

I tell it all to Lucien. He's stretched to the max on the furry white couch in his mother's red apartment, looking like something you'd want to paint. Low-slung jeans and the black-on-black kimono, open and almost falling off, so I see the whole smooth front of him all the way down to his pouty-looking outie and the blue tattoo of the Algiz rune. He's drawing in his sketchbook—*scratch, scratch, scratch*—but I know that he is listening as he murmurs "Nazi" under his breath in his French so-sexy accent, his nostrils flaring, wide and black.

"Dad's not that bad," I'm about to say, but Esme's back, dangling a pair of shoes. She's been foraging through Lucien's mother's closet again. "I'm going to borrow these," she says. Silvery snakeskin. Four-inch heels.

Lucien yawns. Asks if she's put the others back. "My mother noticed them gone, you know."

"I didn't take them. Mitra did."

Not a likely story. Esme lies like others breathe. And Mitra's more into boots.

"Well, somebody has to put them back. Also, *Maman* requests that you all stay out of her private realm. She's going to put on a lock."

"Blah, blah, blah," says Esme. Her skirt's so tight, the V of her thong shows through in back as she bends to put on the shoes. "Your mum just loves that we raid her stuff. It makes her feel very cool."

Lucien twirls his pencil. "Tessa's father—*dad*, I mean—says she can't see me anymore. What do you think of that?"

Esme jumps like someone's stuck her with a pin. The bangles clang on her bony wrists.

"I don't get it. What do you mean?" She's tall as a tree in the spiky heels.

"Tes . . . sa's dad . . . does . . . not . . . want . . ." He drags it out as if Esme's deaf and a hundred years old.

"Can someone really do that? I never heard of such a thing."

Lucien laughs. "Isn't she precious, Tess?" he says. "You'd think she was raised by wolves."

"I don't see *your* mummy here too much." Esme's English. Says "mummy" a lot. She rolls her eyes at Lucien. "She doesn't even notice when the clothes in her closet disappear."

"You take her *clothes*?" This is news to Lucien, who up till now thought it was only shoes. He goes back to the subject of my dad and tries to explain to Esme that certain parents in the world do, in fact, tell their kids who to see or not. This doesn't compute in Esme's brain. She sinks to the white alpaca next to my boyfriend's feet. "Boyfriend," I've just begun to say.

"Bizarre," she comments, mystified, and fiddles with his toes. This I hate. Her bony fingers are limp with rings. Peridot and turquoise. Some great big diamond with a crack. Lucien's toes are beautiful. The bottoms of his feet are smooth. Petal soft, the color of a flower tea. "Why don't they like poor Lucien? He's a sweet little boy. Wouldn't hurt a fly."

"That tickles, Esme. Get the hell off."

"But why?" she coos. "Just tell me why." It's hard to look at Esme. Her beauty messes up my head. Her china-blue eyes don't match the darkness of her skin. Her "mum's" Malaysian, so she says. But no one's ever seen her mum, so the story's probably bogus too. Her height comes from her father (this part Lucien says is true), a red-faced Brit, thin as a flagpole and just as stiff. Esme's hair is long and white. Cornsilk strands that fly in her face. I bought some bleach, but Lucien said *Don't touch your hair.* He loves my looks, he tells me. So fresh and squeaky American-clean.

"Her father thinks I bring the marijuana." "Marie Juan," it sounds like, like the name of an exotic girl.

"So what. Who cares."

"Well, it isn't me. I wouldn't share my stash like that."

"Don't put yourself down. You're very kind."

"Try to stay focused, Esme sweet."

"Well, who made it up, this rumor, when everyone knows it's Wid?"

"They talk on Sunday at the church."

"What church?" says Esme, wide-eyed.

"All the Americans go to church. And when it's over they have *café*—"

"And doughnuts?" says Esme brightly. "I had an American doughnut once—"

"Hopeless," says Lucien close to my ear.

"You Americans always hate the French. And I know why," says Esme. "You're jealous because they speak so nice and they make soufflés and those chilly little aspic things."

"What chilly little aspic things?"

"Those things with the *tomatoes*. Lucien knows the things I mean." Esme stretches out her legs and stares at the snakeskin shoes. Then flashing back to me again:

"Can't you just tell them it isn't true? That the little Dutch boy sells the weed?"

"You really want her to rat on Wid?" Lucien intervenes for me. He's stippling with his pencil now, putting angry eyebrows on my dad. Esme shrugs.

"Will your dad try to have him ganked, you think?"

"*Vous êtes très drôle,*" says Lucien, which means "you are very funny," though Esme is not laughing, not even a smile on her spaced-out face.

"Doesn't he work for the CIA?"

Lucien whispers, "FBI." I'd asked him to keep this to himself. My dad doesn't advertise that fact; people in the Bureau don't. Not that it's some big secret. For three months now, since we moved to Argentina, he's been stationed at the embassy—the "legal attaché," he's called—with his weird little dweeb assistant,

Jer, formally known as Jerry. We're supposed to say he works for "Justice" if anyone asks. That's *Department* of Justice, by the way, not the whole ideal.

Esme springs up. "Does he have a gun?"

"Go home," said Lucien, waving her off.

"No, really, does he? I bet he does." She clomps back and forth across the room, testing out the shoes. "Anyway, I guess I'll go. I know you really want me to. Plus Gash is taking me out tonight."

"How can you stand that scary old scag?" Gash is gross, but I'm glad we've stopped talking about my dad.

"Gash is an icon. An *icon*, love. He changed the world of rock."

"He's a dirty old man, is what he is."

"He isn't dirty. He bathes a lot. Sometimes several times a day and with soap that's made by monks. Anyway, who cares. Gash and I have fun. We play this game—I call him 'Daddy' when we go out. At Christmastime, he's taking me to Italy."

"If you live to be twenty, Esme, it will be a miracle. *Arrivederci.* Blow a kiss." Esme smiles, teetering slightly in the heels. She opens the door and tosses puffs of air at us.

"Find who has my mother's clothes!" Lucien hollers after her. Her footsteps clatter in the hall. It sounds like she's walking back and forth, breaking in the shoes. Seconds pass and we hear the elevator doors and the fading hum as the big brass cage lowers from the penthouse floor.

I turn to look at Lucien to ask him again not to mention my father's job. But then I don't, because he's put down the pad and pencil with the portrait of my Nazi dad. He's smiling too, the dimples dark at the ends of his mouth. That's what I fell in love with first—those shady wounds at the corners there. He was standing in front of a painting by Michelangelo—a poster, that is, on the wall of the art room at our school. His full-lipped mouth looked just like the painted angel's, and I knew I was going to kiss it soon. That was just two weeks ago—well, sixteen days and a couple of hours—yet I feel like I've always known that mouth, tilting now in the slow, faint smile that's only meant for me.

"What are we going to do?" I ask.

"It's so sexy when you're serious. Everything dire and *ter-ee-bul*."

"My dad isn't kidding, Lucien. We really have to make a plan."

"Tessa. *Belle. Ma Tessa.*" His voice is soft and sibilant. And already I feel the slow, hot dip just hearing the way he says my name with the *belle* in between, which in French, you know, means beautiful. "We'll work it out. We'll sneak around."

"You don't know my dad—"

"We'll make up stories. Little lies. You'll say that you're at Esme's house. Or Mitra's place. Who cares? Your father can't come to school with you or follow you around all day."

"He knows when I'm lying. He has a gift."

"Don't worry, Tess. I'll teach you how to do it. How to lie so good that nobody sees it in your eyes." He reaches out and takes my hand. I forget about Dad as he draws me down on top of him. The silk kimono slips away, my face falling into the warm, dark slot beside his own. He talks in French against my hair as if what he needs to say to me can only be said in the language that came first to him.

So we make our plan: We'll lie and fake. We'll make up stories and sneak around. "It might be fun," he whispers. Like Esme pretending she's Gash's daughter, calling him "Daddy" wherever they go, playing their game in the secret dark of clubs and bars. We could go to Alibi Alice too. She's a girl at school who, for money, will fix up everything. "She's an entrepreneur," says Lucien. Before I leave we drink some port. I don't really like the taste of it, but I love to hold the tiny cut-glass thimbles he takes from the Chinese cabinet. Solange, Lucien's mother, is a cultural attaché and has things from all around the world. We sit on the floor on the Turkish rug.

He signs the drawing of my dad. He tears it out and I put it in my sketchbook, in between the pages, the way you'd press a flower.

"Drawings," whispers Lucien, "are more intense than photographs. They're the actual lines that the person has made. With the impulse of his nerves and touch." When I look at this drawing years from now—when I'm old, he says, "an old, old girl in a red wool cap"—I'll remember this afternoon.

The drawing doesn't look like Dad. It doesn't look like anyone. But already I know the other part's true. The part about remembering.

I leave Lucien's and I walk so fast. I cross the twelve lanes of Avenida 9 de Julio in one spurt—not even a pause at the final curb. After being with Lucien, I can fly, even with my school books and the clunky sack of art supplies. In only minutes I'm at Plaza San Martín, the sprawling park with its ombu trees and the statue of the saint. He's up on a horse, a warrior saint. People are strewn all over the grass in the last fast-fading spots of sun. It's chilly still, but the Santa Rosa winds have come, and soon it will be summertime. Along the plaza's shady edge, the old stone mansions—San Martín Palace, the Plaza Hotel—catch late-day light on their pale facades.

Tourists are streaming out of Calle Florida onto the streets and into the park. They move in groups, heavy with their shopping bags. You always know which ones they are. The real porteños, which is what they call the natives of Buenos Aires, are dark and sleek, gliding quickly through their world in clicking leather boots. Even the moms are totally hot. They're thin and really elegant, nothing like the moms back home in Annandale.

The breeze runs through their long black hair as they chatter away in small, tight groups, their smocked little kids in tow.

When I'm skimming across the plaza and I see these young and sexy moms, I pretend that I am one of them. It's stupid, I know; I used to do the same with Mike—pretend I was old and married. But now it's Lucien instead, and in my dream I'm dropping my kids at private school and heading off with the other moms to some chic and intimate café.

The fantasies follow me all the way home—on the train from Retiro Station to the leafy suburb where I live. Though the neighborhood is full of houses and lawns and trees, it isn't like the suburb of Virginia where my family has always lived. The houses here are very close; the roofs of some of them even touch. They're huge and tall and fortresslike, shaded with enormous trees—linden, plane, and the *gomas* with their polished leaves. The private spaces are in the back, sheltered from the world. On weekends the voices of the neighbors filter through the walls of hedge, soft and indistinct. The air is spiked with the scent of their *asados*, a smoky blend of fragrant wood and roasting meat that gets into your memory.

Along the way are the tiny booths where the *vigilancia* hang out. Every block has a private guard to watch for crooks and kidnappers. Kidnapping is a danger here. Or so they say at the embassy. I wave to our *vigilancia*. It's Luis today with his sleepy dog.

Inside my house I notice right away that everything's superclean. It's always pretty clean, of course, now that we have a maid, but today I can smell the lemon wax hanging in the air. There are flowers too, and piles of little napkins with BIENVENIDOS scrawled on top. With a thud I remember it's Chatter Night. That's what they call their boring little parties when "the embassy folk," as my dad likes to say, come over to "shoot the breeze." It's not a festive gathering—just a bunch of military guys and Immigration and that whole bunch who are stationed at the embassy. When Dad first proposed these Chatter Nights, I thought they might be interesting. But mostly they talk about office stuff and what's on sale at the embassy store. I know what stuff they talk about because on Chatter Night Dad always makes me serve hors d'oeuvres. It's only for half an hour, but I hate it like crazy anyway. He likes to show off his family—now that he's in our midst again.

My mom's in the kitchen with Nidia. I hardly recognize her these days. Since coming to Buenos Aires, she's been totally transformed. She plays tennis with friends and goes out to lunch, and once a week some cutie guy from Rio gives her a massage. Her skin is tanned, which sets off the highlights in her hair. Next thing you know, she'll be doing something to her face.

"Tessa, hi," she greets me, glancing up from the pigs-in-a-blanket all ready to go. Nidia smiles and waves at me. She's wiping glasses with a towel.

"Hi," I say.

"So, where've you been?"

"Santa Fe. Looking at clothes."

"Who with?"

"You know. The girls."

"Was Cathy there?"

"No, not today." My mom's a fan of Cathy, who could win a prize for wholesomeness. Her father works for State. Mom starts to make her marinade—jam and Gulden's mustard that she buys at the embassy store each week. Into this she drops the cut-up hot dogs yuck and sets it on the stove. The guests just love it, she always claims. It makes them think of home. When Lucien's mom has parties, a Peruvian maid serves sautééd oysters on a pick and marinated scallops that slide from a rippled seashell right into your mouth. I was there one night for a minute or two.

"Get anything nice?" my mom asks next. And I almost forget where I said I was. I'm not the best of liars yet.

"Nah," I say. And reaching for a piece of cheese: "This thing tonight. Do I really have to stay and serve?"

"Oh, Tess, come on. It's just for half an hour." The marinade looks horrible. Queasy brown with little red franks.

"Nobody cares if I'm there or not."

"Your father cares. It's important to him." She lets out a sigh as if I'm really wearing her out. As if all I do is sap her strength. "He doesn't ask very much of you."

This isn't true. She knows it too. Since Dad's been living with us again, he's been asking quite a lot of me. In addition to asking for perfect grades and excellent "comportment" (since now we're like ambassadors), he's asked me not to see Lucien. He's *told* me, that is. It was not a request.

But of course, I don't get into that. Mom's trying to deal with Dad herself. It can't be easy having him in charge again after two whole years of running the show while he was sta-tioned in Colombia. Mom didn't want to move the family to Bogotá so we saw him on weekends twice a month. We got used to doing things our way.

I look at Mom and decide not to make a fuss tonight. All right already, I'll serve hors d'oeuvres. I'll get A's in school and be a model citizen. I'll do every stupid thing they want—except stop seeing Lucien.

III

Up in my room I flick on my computer. My phone buzzes from deep in my bag.

I can still taste u.

My fingers wobble on the screen.

Is it good? I ask. I kind of suck at talk like this.

Mmmmmm.

What u doin?

Thinking of u.

Me 2.

Of u?

No. U.

TB.—That means *très bien*. Sexy, right?

Going out?—I punch, though I know he is.

Meeting G. Sneak out w us.

Ha.

See u tomorrow. Kiss.

Kiss. B good.

I kiss my iPhone and put it down.

Still smiling, I walk into my closet. It's almost as big as my room back home.

Sometimes I just hang out in here, drifting around or gazing up at the big, round skylight overhead, patterned with leaves and grayish jacaranda limbs. I grab my dress. It's the coolest thing I've ever owned. Bought it last week with Mitra, Kai, and Esme. They're Lucien's friends and have been here for at least a year, and now I'm sort of in their clique. They took me to a store they know where all the kids from Europe shop. The price of the dress was my whole net worth. I didn't care. I've never had a dress like this. It looks like a painting by Georgia O'Keeffe, gray with a giant purple rose. The bra-like straps are really thin and the cloth is so light it lifts in the air when I take a breath. I tried it on for Lucien, and he told me to walk around the room so he could draw me wearing it.

Across the room my computer lights up, all purple and blue with my Monet *Water Lilies* screen. On the surface of the lily pond is a message from Norah. Yay! She's the only thing I miss about my former life. Norah—Noree—my bestest friend. We met in first grade while standing on the line for lunch. The rest is history, as they say.

Hey Tess,

I'm bored to death and I hate my life without you here. What's happening with L? Why does your dad hate him so much? Also, when r u going to break it to Mike? I can hardly stand to look at his face. What else. I'm working on a story for the school paper called "Waste in the Cafeteria." Exciting, right? And I cut my hair. I sort of have bangs like a manga chick.

Write back soon. I miss u!

Love ya,
Noreeeeeee

P.S. Pls. b careful whatever u do.

I flick off the computer without opening Mike's email, which sits there in its little slot like an unexploded bomb. My eyes rove slowly over the desk and out the window into the yard. Everything is lush and green though it's only early spring. Clumpy birds of paradise jab the air like long green knives; I can hardly wait for them to bloom, brilliant orange with streaks of blue. There's a little chink in the foliage where our next-door neighbors' house shows through. They're embassy people too—Indians from India—and sometimes I see them in the yard. They hang their bright saris on the clothesline, and at night the smells of their cooking and sounds of their dreamy music come floating through the air.

I have to tell Norah what's going on. The last time I wrote, my dad hadn't yet banned Lucien. Wonder what she'll say to that. Her own dad's even worse than mine. An actual real-life general stationed at the Pentagon. Speaking of dads, I hear my own. He's home from work, his big "hello" bouncing off the walls downstairs. It's almost six. The guests will be here pretty soon.

I glance in the mirror. The dress looks really good on me. It changes my whole body—not that my body's horrible; it's just not special in any way, like Esme's long, brown body is. The thin black straps make my collarbones stand out. Lucien says my collarbone is beautiful. I'd never noticed it before, but now I look at it all the time. I think I'm in love with my collarbone. Lucien likes to kiss it. He plants his mouth lightly on my shoulder, then glides along the edge of bone, nudging the neckline of my shirt, till his mouth slips into the center dip and I feel my pulse against his lips, a bird heartbeat that doesn't stop even as he slides away.

One time he held a mirror and told me to watch as he kissed my throat. After that he gathered my hair and held it up on top of my head. "Keep looking," he said, as he traced his fingers all around those underparts—the shadow behind my earlobe, the dent in the back just under the skull, where the wisps of hair seem like leftover strands from babyhood. It was never, ever like this with Mike.

I take a last look at my dress and me. I pull out the fabric, light as air, and watch it settle back into place. It reminds me of petals, falling, slow motion, out of a tree. Going down the stairs I feel like I am floating. Like I'm the rose on the front of my dress, mysterious and intricate, with secrets in the deepest parts.

IV

Downstairs my whole family is gathered in the living room. My mom's in her Eva Perón apron, firing up the Sterno. My older brother, Bill, is eating a Triscuit, and nine-year-old Tyler is drooling over the pigs-in-a-blanket on the tray. My dad is at the cabinet taking out the Scotch, but when I come in, his head pops up and something happens to his face. It's like someone's just clobbered him with a stick.

"What the—" The words kind of sputter out of his mouth. My mom and Bill both check me out. Six big eyes are staring at my skinny straps. My dad completes his cut-off thought: "—heck have you got on?"

Seconds flip as I turn to find my mother's eyes, which suddenly aren't eyes at all but big, *colossal* olives, like the ones in the little boat-shaped bowls next to the cream-cheese roll-up things. (Everyone loves the "roll-ups" too. It makes them think of home.)

"It's called a dress," I tell him. "It's a famous designer dress, in fact—"

"Well, it looks like underwear to me, and you can't greet guests in your underwear." The silence would be deafening if not for Tyler's giggling at the out-loud mention of "underwear." "Look at her, Nan." My dad spins around to face my mom. "You can't have approved—I know you never saw this dress."

"Oh, Jim," says Mom in that weary tone she's taken to using nowadays. "It's just the style. All the girls wear things like this."

"The *what*—the *style*? You're telling me this is Tessa's *style*?" He turns to Bill. "Do *you* think this is Tessa's style? Be honest, Bill; I want to know. To me it looks like underwear."

My brother shrugs and looks away. As if to say, *What do I know about Tessa's style—or underwear or anything?* He looks like dad's twin, in his khaki pants, creased like a board by Nidia, and his navy Izod shirt. Tyler's giggling again. Will they ever stop saying "underwear"?

Then Dad says in a serious voice, "We have people from Kuwait tonight."

"I don't even want to be here." The words come snapping out of my mouth. "I'd rather serve drinks in a cocktail lounge. At least I'd get some tips." Dad laughs at this. I mean laughs like it's funny, ha, ha, ha. Then he says, in earnest, that I ought to be thrilled to mingle in a crowd like this. He acts as if the Chatter Nights are full of maharajas and exotic heads of state instead of mostly Americans (and, tonight, a lost Kuwaiti) who talk, like I said, about interoffice memos and why the chips from the embassy shop are always a little stale.

Then he says the craziest thing—the craziest thing my dad has *ever* said to me: "What about that yellow dress—the one we bought you in New York? You know, the one with the squiggly trim?"

Even my mom gives him a look like he's lost his mind. "She was ten years old when we bought that dress." I know by my father's goofy face that he still sees me in that lemony dress and anklets, and it makes me want to scream.

"I'll handle this, Jim," Mom tells him next, and she motions for me to go with her. I'm burning up about my dad. I'm sixteen years old and completely in love, and my dad still thinks I'm the girl in a dress that went to Goodwill when I was twelve. It makes me so mad it's hard to breathe. On top of that, I can't believe he said "squiggly trim."

"Come on," says Mom in a gentle voice. She motions for me to go with her. I can hardly think, so I do what she wants and follow her up the stairs. I catch a glimpse of Tyler's face. He's relieved, I can tell, that I didn't answer back to Dad. He hates when we fight. It makes him so nervous he starts to twitch.

Up in my room, my mom says she thinks my dress is nice, just not for tonight, and maybe not when Dad's around. "It's not a big deal. Just put on something else for now."

"It *is* a big deal," I start to explain. "Dad doesn't know what's going on. It's like he's missed the last two years."

"He has," says Mom. "Just give him some time."

"At the rate he's going, he'll never catch up."

Mom smiles as if she understands, but it's clear she doesn't want to talk. "What about that dress with those funky buttons?" She's heading for my closet, and I move to cut her off.

"It's all right. I'll find a dress." I don't want to hurt her feelings, but if she won't take a stand for me, she can't go acting like my friend and rummage through my stuff. At times like this I remember how we were before, and wish my Dad had stayed away.

V

In the next scene I'm walking around the living room in my funky-button dress with a tray of Triscuits and deviled ham. My mom was right; Americans love this crappy food. The army guys really wolf it down. So do the marine guys, who work as guards at the embassy. I like the marine named Carlos. He's cute and kind of nice to me. The Kuwaiti guy is also cute. He's skinny and young with a beautiful face, and is dressed in a long gray robe. He passes on Mom's great hors d'oeuvres. I think he's vegetarian. The rest of them—the State Department and consulate guys are wearing their "casual" uniform: polo shirts and khakis, with serious creases down the front. The kids at school hide their jeans from the crease-mad maids.

My dad's assistant, dweeb of the world, is dressed like all the rest of them, except Jer doesn't button his Izod shirt and his long black chest hair straggles out and tangles in golden chains. From one of the chains hangs a big old cross. Before Jer joined the FBI, he ran some kind of mission that rescued "at-risk youth." He lives with his mother, if you can believe. He brought her to Argentina. She makes red velvet cake and cookies, which he brings into the embassy. After his mother, what Jer loves best is his little black gun. Even now, I can see it strapped around his shin, bulging underneath his pants. My dad doesn't even carry a gun, but Jer, the missionary guy, can't bear to give his up.

"Hey, Tess," says Jer when I offer the tray. "What's the scuttle-butt these days?" What do you say to a question like that? Then Jer asks if the "topping" has any mushrooms. Yeah. Deviled ham *aux Champignons*. He's allergic, he says, and "that's no joke." Bill, on the other hand, takes two at a time and scarfs them down. He doesn't have to serve hors d'oeuvres. He's just required to hang around and make sure that everyone has a full glass or a beer bottle in his hand.

Bill actually wants to be here. Bill wants to grow up and *become* my dad—finish college, go to law school, and join the FBI—so he loves to hang around all night chewing the fat with the personnel from DOD (Department of Defense), DEA (Drug Enforcement Agency), and all the rest of that alphabet soup. He already sort of looks the part with his muscled physique and stubby hair. I like him anyway, I guess. He works for Volun-teers for Peace and took six months off from college to help in Guatemala, which I think is really nice. (Though I wish he could have stuck up for my dress.)

My younger brother, Tyler, always has fun at Chatter Night. He likes it best when the military people show up in their uni-forms. "Hi, sir (or ma'am)," he greets them, staring up at their decorated chests. "My name is Tyler." He likes to salute, which drives the female militia wild.

Speaking of female militia, my dad's secretary comes over and takes one of the delicacies from my tray. She's skinny and old, but from what I'm told is a model of efficiency. "Hi there, Tessa. Pretty dress. I've been strolling around admiring your artwork." She has steely hair that holds the shape of the circular curlers she wears at night. The ruffle of her starched white blouse goes halfway up her neck. "I really like that landscape there." She points to a watercolor of George Washington's big white house. I did it one time when Mike and I and Noree went to Mount Vernon for the day. I'm sort of embarrassed to look at it now, and I told my parents I wanted them to take it down, along with my other art class stuff—the vases of flowers, the apples and pears.

"Thanks, Mrs. McKnight," I say.

"You can call me Mary," she tells me next. Which I know I'll never do. I'll just call her nothing from here on in. "Have you done any paintings since coming to Buenos Aires?" She's looking at a stupid picture of a tree on the wall above the couch.

"Not yet," I say. Though I really have. One day Lucien and I filled five huge canvases with paint. No trite little scenes. Just pure, unmixed color. We used up tubes of oil paint. It was intense, it really was. It changed the way I see. I think I'd die if Lucien saw the crummy artwork I used to do. Though he never will, because Lucien's never coming here. He'd probably find my house surreal. The curtains and lamps and the matching pillows on the chairs. I ease away from Mrs. McKnight. My tray needs a refill, if you can believe.

In the kitchen Nidia smiles at me. She's young and pretty and has two little kids whose pictures she's always showing me. It can't be too great being a maid, yet she's always in a cheery mood. Sometimes I try to talk Spanish with her, but I'm really not too good at it. She comprehends that I need more hors d'oeuvres.

Finally it's over and I'm back in my room. I try to call Lucien, but he's not picking up. He goes out every night, and his mother never bothers him. I'm jealous, of course, but I try to put it out of my mind. I do some homework. Study for my history test. Take a shower and read in bed. Text a message to Lucien. I do everything but open Mike's email, which is starting to rot inside my in-box. I'm awful, I know, but I just can't seem to read it. Without even looking I know what it says.

Hey, Tess. Where are you? Some stuff about how he misses me. Some other stuff about football games. He's on the team again this year. A couple of lines about our school and college acceptances coming up. He's planning to go to Georgetown. The following year I was supposed to join him there. I think we thought we'd go away to college and end up getting married like high school sweethearts in a book. Mike's always been really good to me. Kind of the protective type. I really thought I loved him too. But now that I'm with Lucien, I know I never did. I hate to hurt him, I really do. But I just don't feel it anymore.

VI

Lucien's apartment is blurry and dark, the only light from the dim Moroccan lanterns, indigo-blue and saffron and a burning poppy red. Out on the terrace the starry points of cigarettes merge with the city's twinkling lights, and the air has a thrill I can't explain. I'm high on wine and a pill that Esme gave to me.

Half the people I don't know. There are kids from school—Wid and Kai and Mitra and other kids whose parents hold diplomatic posts. No one is American. There are also some sleazy-looking guys who might be from the street. They have greasy hair and darting eyes that always flick back to Esme's legs. Esme's really out of it, lying on the furry couch, her feet on the silver table where she's dropped the shiny pills. They look like beads or candy, blue and purple, red and green. Lucien's head is on my lap and I'm running my fingers through his hair. His curls are so soft, yet they spring right back when I stretch them straight and let them go. I'm wearing my dress and it's all bunched up beneath his head. Kai comes in and plunks down next to Esme.

"So, Tess," she says, "where do your parents think you are?" She's drinking beer from a small pink glass that's shaped like a bell.

"We're using Alice," Lucien says, stirring slightly on my lap.

"Alice who?"

"Alice the Canadian."

"You're kidding me."

"No. Why would I?"

"I wouldn't even talk to her. Sometimes I'm next to her in gym, and she smells like—"

"Don't be mean," I murmur.

"Yes, don't be mean," says Lucien. "She serves a purpose in this world."

Kai throws back her mop of hair, which always lands just right. Dark red waves at the edge of her eye.

"What purpose does smelly Alice serve?"

"For fifty US dollars she'll be the place you're supposed to be." Lucien eases upward, and my lap is suddenly bare and cold. I pull the dress down to cover my thighs. "But she only does English-speaking jobs."

"You actually paid her money?"

Lucien nods. "We're trying her out."

"Weird," says Kai, leaning forward to look more closely at the pills. Then: "Where does Esme get this junk?"

"It isn't junk." Esme suddenly resurrects. "They're beautiful jewels from Gash." She passes a blue one over to me.

"OxyContin. Take it, Tess. It makes you nice and numb." I slip the pill into the slot inside my bag. I'm starting a small collection there.

"Where's Gash tonight?" Kai queries.

"I think he's with Evangeline."

"Who the hell is that?"

"She used to play drums in Gash's band."

"Gross," says Kai. "She must be old." She adds something in French to Lucien—Kai is Dutch, speaks half a dozen languages—which he keeps all to himself. At least the greasies have moved away and aren't staring at Esme's legs. I ask who they are and Lucien says they came with Wid. Or someone. Then he says he's hungry. To me he whispers, "Let's find some food."

In the kitchen everything feels very French. There are bottles of wine on wire racks and all kinds of herbs hanging upside down. We aren't there to look for food. He backs me up against the refrigerator door and kisses me on the neck. My skin goes shivery under his mouth. He kisses my throat and the collarbone he loves so much. Tonight he doesn't say it, though. My knees feel weak and I lean for support against the door. His fingers slip under the straps of my dress. He pulls them off my shoulders and looks without touching for a while.

His eyes are so big. So damp and dark, and tonight they're slightly ringed with red. I'm not sure what he took or smoked. I know he drank a little wine; I taste it when he kisses me.

"Come to my room," he whispers. He takes my hand and I

go along. We pass through the red, red living room. One wall is made of windows, and beyond the glass the diamonds wink and the lights reflect, melting color in the air. I'm floating away and my heart is beating in my ears.

We sink to his bed. Everything's black and slippery. Everything seems to be made of silk. The sheets are cool and the pillow is slick on the back of my neck. He slips off his shirt and he's silk underneath. The most beautiful, tawny silk there is. Through my half-closed eyes I see his face as he eases himself on top of me.

"Don't be afraid," he whispers.

There's a mirror beyond him on the wall. It's totally smashed, cracked like a mosaic, and vaguely I think, *He did that, too.* He's so close he blurs, and he looks like someone I don't know. Or he doesn't look like anyone. Just a trembling shape in the dark and light. No, that's not right. He isn't trembling at all. I'm the one who's trembling. That's why he says *Don't be afraid.*

My dress with the rose is slipping off and the air is very cold. The strangest scene floats into my mind. It's winter in the picture. Snow and frozen birdbaths and bushes of thorns with bright red rose hips on the limbs, which I suddenly feel at the tip of my breasts. My nipples are hard red rose hips. I picture them sprouting under his lips.

If I open my eyes I see the ceiling high above and an edge of wall where his giant orange painting hangs. I love him, I know, but I can't say the words and my brain is doing funny things. It's like I'm there but not. So then I stop trying to figure it out.

He's speaking in French whatever. He's kissing the edge of every rib. Then *bang, bang, bang!* Someone's pounding on the door. Kai pokes in and says that Lucien's mother's home.

By the time we get out to the living room, everyone's gone or going. Someone smart has grabbed the pills, but the place is still a mess. Solange's jacket is hanging from her shoulder, and her Louis Vuitton is on the floor, toppled where she let it drop. She has thick dark hair that curves around her shoulders, and she keeps on pushing it out of the way as she whips her startled head around. The minute Lucien comes into view she starts babbling in French at him. She's all out of breath; and she's very beautiful angry like that. There's a spot of red on each of her cheeks under those high, tipped bones. She isn't kidding all the same, wringing her hands and gasping as if she can't get air.

"Go," says Lucien to me.

"Yes, go," she says in English. I wonder if she has asthma and is having an attack. There's only Esme, Kai, and me. It's really bad and awkward. And I feel like I'm skulking out the door.

Down in the lobby, Kai pretends that we don't care and laughs in the *portero*'s face. She dials on her cell for a *remise*, a private car, that shows up a few minutes later. We all pile in and she gives Esme's address in Palermo Chico. Kai's in charge because Esme's still not functional, and her Spanish is good compared to mine.

To me she says, "You were going to stay there, weren't you?" I nod my head; yeah, that was the plan—though I suddenly can't remember ever actually making it. "Well, we're going to stay at Esme's now." I'm shaking still and I'm not sure why. The fuzzy buzz of the pill's gone flat.

VII

Esme's street is beautiful. The trees are thin and lacy, and their shadows look like filigree. In the townhouse next to Esme's, a party is still going on. We can hear the hum of voices and the clink of glass and silverware. It must be nearly three o'clock. We climb the steps to enter, and Kai has to dig out Esme's key from the mess inside her purse. When she opens the door, a smell floats out in the chilly air. Garbage, smoke, and something I know but just can't name. Something that almost makes me retch. I don't want to go in. It feels all wrong. It feels like a place I dreamed of once. When we step inside, there's a flurry of movement like swirling wind. And then I see the cats.

"God," says Kai. "It's worse than the last time I was here. You need to fumigate this place."

"Welcome," says Esme, loopylike. Four gray cats slink over to say hello to her. She answers *"Meow,"* sounding just like one of them.

We sit in a filthy living room. The couches are made of charcoal-colored leather with scratch marks all along the arms.

The long glass tables are covered with empty bottles, take-out cartons, and ashtrays full of who knows what. The ceiling goes up two stories high, and across the room huge windows open to a terrace. There are big stone sculptures and giant pots. Everything in the pots is dead. It's creepy and beautiful in its way.

"That was funny," Esme says. "Solange popping in the way she did. Everyone in a daft stampede." She kicks off a pair of stolen shoes.

"Glad you think so," Kai replies, throwing some clothing onto the floor to clear a place to sit. "She wasn't supposed to come home tonight."

"What do you think will happen?" I ask. I try to get comfortable on the couch, but I don't even want to touch it. A cat is staring into my face.

"To Luce, you mean?" Kai shrugs. "Solange will be mad for a day or two. She may even threaten to send him back—"

"Back where?"

"To France. Where his father lives."

"Would she really do that?"

"Yes, of course. She threatens him all the time. Though she never actually follows through. I'm sure you've seen the way she spoils her baby boy."

"I've only met her once before. And we hardly even talked."

"You'd like her," says Kai. "Everybody likes Solange. Which brings me to a question: What's the problem with your dad?" I don't say anything to that, and Kai goes on as if she's talking to herself. "It's not like Lucien's off the streets. Solange is really classy. She's the cultural attaché to France." I still don't speak, and then Kai asks, "Isn't your dad in the FBI? I mean, isn't he basically a cop?"

It's weird how I don't know what to feel. I suddenly want to defend my dad. He's not a cop, I want to say—I didn't know Dutch people used that word—he's also a lawyer and speaks a couple of languages (not that she'd be impressed by that). I'm also surprised she knows he's with the FBI. Word really seems to get around.

Kai screws up her face. "So what's the problem, Tessa? Why does your dad hate Lucien?"

"People say that he's selling drugs."

"That's it?" Kai laughs. "You Americans are hilarious. You can buy a gun in a grocery store, some crazy kid can shoot up an entire school, but a stick of weed—oh my God, call Interpol." I don't know what she's talking about. Maybe she's thinking of Columbine, which I think they made a movie of, but it's really late and I don't have the strength to get all patriotic now.

On the other couch, Esme suddenly comes to life.

"She plays the drums—Evangeline. *Boom, boom, boom.* With those little sticks." She must have had a dream. She's blinking her eyes and looks confused. "Anyway, I'm going to bed. You can sleep in any room you want." She climbs to her feet and wobbles, then staggers down a darkened hall. Most of the cats follow right behind her, their skinny, grayish bodies making a ghostly *whoosh*.

"Shit," says Kai. "Like I'd ever sleep in one of her beds. I should've just gone home."

"Why didn't you, then?"

"I was worried for her. She's really stoned."

"Does she really live here by herself?" I glance around at the piles of trash all over the floor. "Who pays the rent and the bills and stuff?"

"Her dad, I guess. But he lives with some woman in Uruguay. She says she has a mother, but look around. Does that seem possible to you?"

"What about a maid?"

"Gash fired the maid. Afraid that she might turn him in. Now and then he calls some people in to clean."

"Wow" is all I can think to say. Kai stretches out on the leather couch.

"There's a bathroom somewhere down the hall. It's scary, but the water works. I wouldn't go into the kitchen, though." She closes her eyes, and I know she's already half asleep. I wish that I could be like her. Just shut out the world and disappear. But I'm weird when it comes to grossness. I could never join the Volunteers like my brother did this summer, and live in some place where there aren't any bathrooms and the roosters and chickens sleep in the house. I sort of lean back and flex my legs, knocking some magazines onto the floor. It's dim in the room, and one of the cats has stayed behind. He's perched on the back of a nearby chair, watching me like a guard. The light in his eyes is funny. It's really like light. Like there's some kind of beam inside his head.

I guess I doze off. Because then I'm awake. For a minute I think I might have died and ended up in hell. The worst part is,

I have to use the bathroom. I'm scared about that. And I'm also scared of getting up. What if the cat attacks me? He looks like he would if I moved too fast. I think about trying to hold it in. And I do, for a while, until I can't. I walk down the hall where Esme went. It's dark and cool, and something keeps crunching under my feet. I'm glad I've left my shoes on. To my right I see an open door. I reach inside and flick on a light. It's a really giant bedroom, totally trashed like the living room. Bed unmade and covered with clothes. Glasses and dishes all over the place. It smells of dirty laundry and old, disgusting food. In the next room, Esme's sleeping. There's a bluish glow seeping through the windows, and I see her on the bed, surrounded by the cats. She's all splayed out, still wearing her clothes, but her skirt's hiked up and her legs look skinny and weird, like sticks. With her long white hair twirling out around her head, she looks like a broken Barbie doll some spoiled girl has thrown away. Against the wall is a blue guitar plugged into a box. GASH, it says on the guitar in a red and yellow scrawl.

When I find the bathroom, I almost throw up. It's full of kitty litter trays, but they're so full of cat crap that the cats, I guess, are too grossed out to use them and just go anywhere they want. I don't blame them, either. I don't want to sit on the toilet seat. I hurry up, my eyes half closed.

And then I see the boots. They're cowboy boots, electric blue like his old guitar, with swirly stitches in black and red. It's the pointy toes that get me. After that I can't stop thinking of Gash's horny-old-man feet. He's been in this room, peed in this very toilet. And I have to get out before I really and truly puke. As I turn on the water to wash my hands, the fattest cockroach I've ever seen goes streaking across the sink.

Forget about falling asleep again. I sit on the couch and wait and pray for day to come. The sky is getting paler and the sculptures on the terrace glow, but it seems to take forever for the light to filter into the house. A bird has been chirping for nearly an hour, and I hate his cheery guts. I feel like I'll never be cheery again. I'm jealous of that bright, clean bird waking up and feeling good, singing on some sweet, green branch. I want to go home like you can't believe.

VIII

I'm basking in a patch of sun that streams through the stained-glass windows. The green of the glass looks liquidy; Jesus's robe and the flock of sheep are a soft and furry white. I'm sleepy and warm, and everyone is singing, *"Come, my Lord, no longer tarry, Take my ransomed soul away."* I'm thinking of food, the crumb cakes and cherry Danish, and the *café con leche* soon to be served in the quaint little breakfast room next door.

To my left is Tyler, trying to follow the words of the song. His hair's still damp, drying into the hard little ridges my mom always makes with the morning comb. She's on the other side of me, smelling faintly of *L'Aire du Temps*, and next to her stands Dad. Bill's on the end near Tyler, so we're one big happy family for everyone to see. My dad is singing really loud.

Later in the breakfast room, we all stand around the paper-covered tables, drinking coffee and eating cake. Everyone speaks English. It's like being in Virginia, except that we're not. We're in Buenos Aires, in the ivy-twined suburban church where all the American "expats" go. There are Brits here too, and lots of people from Canada; it's the favorite Anglo church in town. At least it's not Jer's church of choice.

Today I actually don't mind. I'm still recuperating from Friday night at Esme's house. I took three hot showers on Saturday and thought about burning my big rose dress. Dad would be really pleased about that.

I wander around, talking to some kids from school. To Cathy, whose father works for State, to Maureen, whose dad is army, and to Greg, whose mom does something with INS. Cathy's the one my mom adores. *"Why don't you call up Cathy Blaine?" "That Cathy's so cute. Do you ever talk?"* I say hello to Alice, fat and friendless Alice, who charged me fifty dollars (Lucien actually paid her) to use her as an alibi.

"Was it fun?" she asks, her mouth overflowing with half-chewed crumbs.

"It was all right. No big deal." I feel like it's smarter to play things down so she doesn't up her rates.

"Your boyfriend's cute," she tells me next. *"Ooh la la. A Frenchy, right?"* She takes another chomp of cake, powdered sugar sticking to her puffy lips. I feel sort of bad that she's such a mess and that all her friends are make-believe. Across the room my dad is chatting with her mom. They look like twins, Alice and her pasty mom, who's also chowing down some cake. Compared to her, my mom looks good. I mean, really good. I look at her now, talking away with the "embassy wives," and she hardly even looks like Mom. She's slim and tan. And whenever she moves, sunlight hits the pale, new highlights in her hair. I doubt they'd even know her in the supermarket back at home.

"Yikes," I say to Alice. "Should my dad be talking to your mom?"

"It's covered," she assures me. "My parents were out playing Trivial Pursuit Friday night. I told them yesterday morning that you stayed over. And I messed up a couple of extra towels. Don't worry, Tessa, I'm good at this. Satisfaction guaranteed." She offers another crumby grin.

IX

After church I'm up in my room, relaxing. The sun's shining in, and it's nice and warm. There's the weekend smell of wood smoke and the faintest sounds of a get-together in someone's yard. I'm lying back against a mound of pillows, and texting away with Lucien.

U alright? he asks me first.

Yeah. U?

I good.

Your mom still mad?

Someone broke some old limoges.

Some what?

Limoges. An ugly vase.

How did it happen?

I don't know. When can I see u? I want to finish what we began.

Yeah me 2.

Know what I mean?

Yes I know.

It's hard to wait. It's really HARD.

My stomach does a loopy dip. I don't know what to say to that.

It hurts, he writes. And I actually have to catch my breath. I stare at a painting on the wall. I did it myself. *Water Lilies After Monet.* It got me an A in art last year. I'm thinking of this and trying to find some hot response when both my parents come into the room. They don't even knock, so I'm pretty sure this can't be good. Alice's face seems to float across the lily pads. SATISFACTION GUARANTEED on the surface of the pond. I type one word to Lucien and pray that he understands.

DAD!!!!

X

You can probably figure out the rest. Through chomps of cake in the breakfast room, Alice's mom somehow managed to tell my dad that on Friday night I "couldn't have possibly" slept at their house. When they got home, she'd peeked into her daughter's room and Alice was all alone. Her mom just figured our plans had changed, and never even mentioned it—until, I guess, she and my dad started chatting it up.

They're standing there together—my parents—and I feel defenseless on the bed.

"Where were you Friday night?" says Dad.

I answer the lamest thing on earth. "I wasn't anywhere," I say. And I'm wishing that it were possible. That a person (me) could actually not be anywhere. Especially not here.

"Where were you?" asks Mom in a softer voice, pretending I haven't answered yet.

"I spent the night at Esme's house."

"So you lied," says my dad, "to your mother and me." I think that's kind of obvious, and I sort of just nod my head.

"I didn't hear you. What did you say?"

"I said, I lied." Which is actually a lie itself. Since I hadn't said a thing.

"Was that French boy there?"

"No," I say. And that's the truth.

"What about her parents?"

"What?"

"Esme's parents. Were they home?"

Since my Dad's been back I've been noticing things I don't think I ever saw before. At least, I don't remember them from before he went away. Like this thing with his eyes, which was happening again right now. First they go glassy around the rims, and the white parts get shiny and really hard. The glaze creeps slowly over the blue to the mean little bull's-eye pupils, and before you know it, both his eyes have turned to ice and hardly look like eyes at all. I glance at Mom. She's mad at me too, but I have the sense that she knows about the frozen eyes. That she's seen them and felt it for herself.

"Tessa," she says. "Were either of Esme's parents there?"

"No," I answer. "They're never there." I'm trying to deflect, of course.

"What do you mean?"

"I mean that no one's ever there. Kai and I—well, we didn't want her to be alone."

"You mean to say she lives by herself? How old is that girl? Is she even sixteen?"

"I don't know," I tell her, and Mom starts looking real upset.

"Poor child," she says. "And I don't mean you." She turns to my dad. "Maybe we ought to *do* something. Intervene or—" She'd call the police if she knew about Gash.

"Right now my only concern is Tess." Dad turns his glass-hard gaze on me. "Do you know why I am so concerned?" I have a few thoughts, but it doesn't matter since I know he's going to fill me in.

"I'm concerned with trust," he tells me. He pauses to let the words sink in. "Trust is everything in life. You trust your friends. You trust the people who work with you. But above all else, you have to trust your family." He sort of wiggles his lower jaw; it's another new habit he has these days, and it makes him look like he's mulling over some dreadful choice. The jaw realigns and on he goes. "Once a trust is broken, well, it's almost impossible to repair. It's hard to believe a person who once lied to you, no matter how meaningless the lie. Like just now. I asked if that boy was there with you, and because you'd already deceived me once, I didn't quite believe you."

"But he *wasn't* there—"

"So you say. But now I cannot trust you. And I won't, I'm sure, for a very long time. Maybe I'll never—"

"All right, Jim," my mother says. "I think that Tessa gets the point."

"I hope she does," he answers. "I certainly hope she does." He turns and starts to leave the room, gets to the door before he whirls around again. "I'm sure she'll also comprehend that there are consequences here." To me he says, "No execution this time, but you're under house arrest."

That's supposed to be funny, believe it or not. It's my dad's weird way of "lightening up" now that the lecture is almost done.

"Two weeks," he says as the look in his eyes begins to thaw. "Your only outings will be to school. To school and back. Do you understand?"

Some hot little ball of anger is forming deep inside my gut, fanning out in bright red waves. Who is he to tell me what I can do or not? In the last two years, Mom never grounded anyone, and if there was a problem, we talked about it and worked things out. He was never a part of any of that, so what makes him think he can just pop in from nowhere and start telling us what to do? I open my mouth to say as much, and Mom steps in between us.

"Jim," she says. "I'd like to talk to Tess alone."

He nods his head, shifting slightly on his feet. For a scary half a second I think he's going to cross the room and kiss me on the forehead like he used to do when I was small and had made all my apologies. But he doesn't, thank God. His FBI instincts are kicking in, and he seems to know that a kiss wouldn't be a good idea. I look at his back as he turns to leave. It's stiff and straight, like there's some kind of rod running up his spine all the way to his head.

XI

Mom plunks down in a nearby chair. She's looking around my bedroom like she's never seen the place before.

"It's beautiful, what you've done here." She picks up a purple pillow and runs her fingers along its edge. This week she did French tips, and her nails have the sheen of pearls. At home she rarely got manicures; the housework always made them chip.

Her eyes keep roving all around. Up the length of watery-looking curtains. Over the rug that I dyed myself to match the blues of Monet's pond. My entire room has a Monet's *Water Lilies* theme. I think she's only noticed now that each of the walls is a slightly different purplish blue, and I've painted vines (which I think are sort of corny now) all along the upper part. A couple of my paintings—the Japanese bird and close-ups of some flowers—are hanging here and there. She stares at the huge hydrangeas, which I did in the style of Georgia O'Keeffe.

"Why is it, Tess, that you haven't done any artwork here? The scenery's so new and different. Our yard alone is full of things that we'd never see in Annandale." Does she really expect an answer? I could ask her a lot of questions too. Why doesn't she play with Tyler the way she used to back home, that crazy freeze tag after school? Or once in a while bake cookies? Or fix my little brother's lunch? But it's probably not the time to ask.

"I painted the ceiling," I say lamely. She has no idea of the stuff I've done with Lucien.

"I mean *paintings*. Artwork. You used to do it all the time. I'd come into the room and there'd you'd be, paint jars all around you, spattered paint on everything. It gave you so much pleasure. I could see it on your face."

I ease my way to the edge of the bed. Plant both feet on solid ground. Mom goes on.

"Something's happened to you, Tess. And I don't just mean the sneaking around. I mean in *you*—in who you are. It's almost as if you've lost your joy. And it makes me very scared."

I could almost burst out laughing. I've *found* my joy, not lost it, and if they'd just let me live my life, I'd probably explode with it.

"Have you heard from Norah?" she asks me next. "New friends are good, but the old ones are best."

"We email every day."

"What about Mike? I know it's hard to keep things going from far away. And boys, let's face it, aren't the best at keeping in touch. But he *is* a great guy, and—" Her words break off and I see the thoughts rolling slowly across her face. "Is that it, Tess? Has Mike started dating someone else? Is that why you're so—"

"I'm not depressed," I finally say. "Well, I am depressed, but it's only because you and Dad won't accept my friends. You've never even met them. People gossip at the church and you just believe whatever they say."

"Tess," says my mom, slipping into her worn-out voice, "your father doesn't do that. He doesn't draw conclusions without sufficient evidence. It's part of his job. It's who he is."

"What are you saying?"

"I'm saying that your father knows. He knows about Wid and some of the other kids at school. I suspect he knows something about your little French boy too."

I hate how she calls him "little" and doesn't use his name. Yet I know if she did—if *Lucien* rolled off her tongue—I'd probably turn ten shades of red and she'd know I was in love with him.

"Darling," she continues—she's only just started to use this word; I think her hairdresser calls her that—"you've lived a different sort of life. Kids like this boy and Esme, well, they come from a different world than you. The French boy's mother is never around. She's some sort of attaché, I think, and the boy is left unsupervised. It's the same thing with that Dutch one—Wid. And as for Esme, I'm appalled. Her parents should be put in jail."

"At least she can choose the friends she wants," I answer in a surly voice. I sound as if I'm twelve.

"We've always let you choose your friends. Norah practically lived with us. And your father and I, we both like Mike. We never curtailed your time with him. So we don't understand

what happened here. Why you don't like the regular kids—
Cathy Blaine or Maureen Fitz—people who are more like *you*."

"What do you mean, who are more like me?" I'm so stunned
it's hard to form the words. "What do I have in common with
Cathy or Maureen—aside from being American?"

"I'm sure you have things in common. Plus, they're very nice
girls, and they're in your class—"

"I thought we came here to meet other kinds of people—
people from different countries, people who *aren't* just like us."

"Yes, of course," Mom answers. "And we want you to make
lots of friends. But that doesn't mean we forget about where we
came from or who we really are."

Now I'm speechless. That's how dumb she thinks I am. I'm so
wowed about living here, so impressed by my newfound friends,
I've forgotten who I am. This makes me so mad I can hardly see.
My vision, I swear, is starting to blur; the scene out the bedroom
window—the trees and branches and spots of sky—is melting
into soup. The other weird thing, which makes me even madder
yet (if such a thing is possible), is the way she keeps saying "we."
We used to mean *us*—her and me. Or her and me and Tyler and
Bill. Suddenly now the "we" just stands for her and Dad, and
doesn't include the rest of us.

She goes on and on in that same solicitous-sounding tone.
*This is an opportunity. We've been hoping for years to get this post.
It's a chance to travel. Learn another language. Live in a beautiful
house with a maid and a cook and a boy who comes to cut the grass.*
My eyes snap back in focus as she finally says what she really

means: "Don't blow it, Tess. I'm serious. It's not just you; it's all of us. I want this for our family, and I won't let you mess it up."

Something inside me starts to sink. It's not about the family, I realize as I watch her face. It's not about Bill or Tyler or me. It's all about Dad—about her and Dad. That's what really matters now. She gets up to leave, and I almost think I'm going to cry. She's standing right there, but it's like she's gone and I miss her already, and I hate my dad for taking her away from me.

XII

I spend half the night with Lucien. First, we text, and I tell him Alice blew it. CALL ME, he writes. I punch the numbers. It's noisy wherever he is, and I take a blanket and go into my closet. I sit in the open doorway. It's strangely bright with moonlight shining into the room.

"Where are you?" I ask.

"I'm at a party with *Maman*. I'm in a closet, actually. Lots of men's black coats."

"I'm in a closet too," I say. Somehow that seems significant, like one more funny thing we share.

"I want my fifty dollars back."

"What?"

"My fifty dollars from Alice the Canadian."

For a minute I don't answer.

"Tessa, hey. Are you all right?"

"I'm not allowed out for two whole weeks. Except to go to school."

"What do you mean?"

"I mean that I'm under house arrest." He laughs a little—at least, it sounds like that to me.

"It isn't funny, Lucien."

"No," he murmurs. "I'm sorry, Tess. But don't you worry, we'll find a way."

"A way to what?"

"A way to be together. We'll sneak out of school and go somewhere."

"They call your house if you cut school."

"Don't worry, *belle*. We'll make a plan." Someone comes into the closet then—the one where he is hiding—and I hear some voices talking in French. It all sounds very friendly. The people are laughing softly, *perdonnez-moi*, as they take their coats.

"I've got to go," he tells me. "I'll think tonight about what to do." For a minute I feel like I'm going to cry. He has no idea what it's like for me. His mother's already forgiven him. It's all in the past, I somehow know. She's brought him to a party. Her friends are joking around with him. I bet she's even forgotten the vase.

"Tessa, sweet, we'll be all right."

"Will we?"

"*Oui.* I promise. Don't be sad. And don't forget—there's our project, too. Tomorrow we will do some work."

"Yeah. Okay." He sounds a kiss, and I picture his mouth, the dark place at the edges, which someday I want to paint.

XIII

It's very early morning. Something bangs. My dad must be going off to work. It's just turning light, so I wonder why he's already up. Then I hear my mother's voice. "Fine thing for you to talk about trust." I hear him trying to hush her. "Wake up the house" are the words I catch, and a door is closed with a muffled, almost gentle sound. I'm mad at them both, and I really don't care about their life.

When I go downstairs he's already gone, and my mom is in the kitchen standing alone in a splotch of sun. Her hair's pulled back, and her eyes are pinched and pink. It looks like she's been crying, and most of my anger melts away.

"Morning," she says, and takes a sip from the mug in her hand. *FIDELITY *BRAVERY. *INTEGRITY. The words encircle the big white mug. (We have lots of crap from the souvenir shop at Quantico.)

"Are you all right?" I ask her, though it's obvious that she's not.

"I'm fine," she says. She's already in her other place—the

place she shares with Dad, not me. It's clear she isn't going to talk. I tell myself that I don't care. If that's what she wants, it's fine with me. I grab a muffin, which Nidia made, and pour a drop of coffee. It's awkward, and I'm glad when Tyler comes into the room. My mom hasn't gotten to his hair—another sign that something's wrong. She pours some cereal into a bowl. As I start to leave the kitchen, she shoots me an unfriendly look. "See you back here at three o'clock." I actually feel like rolling my eyes. The whole thing's so ridiculous.

Tyler and I walk to school, which is only a couple of blocks from home. (It's called an "international" school; most of the foreign diplomats send their sons and daughters here. But English, not Spanish, is spoken in class, and it's named for a US president.)

"Are you in trouble?" Tyler asks as we amble along the tree-lined street.

"Sort of, yeah."

"What did you do?"

"I spent the night at the house of someone they don't like."

"Why?"

"Why what?"

"Why don't they like the person whose house you stayed at?" He's looking at me with his big blue eyes. Like he really wants to understand. But of course I can't explain it to him. Not the whole story, anyway. I tell him I lied and stayed at Esme's instead of where I'd said I would, and that Esme's parents weren't home.

He ponders this. As if I've said something really deep. And then he says, "It's different since we came here, Tess."

"Of course, it is. We're in a different country now. We're on a different continent."

"I mean Mom and Dad. And now you, too. Everybody's different now."

I don't really think I'm different. I think I'm who I always was, only back at home, Dad wasn't there to run my life.

"I want it to be the way it was," Tyler says when I don't respond. "I hate it when everybody fights."

"It's just a transition," I say to him.

"So it's going to get better, Tess?"

"Yes, of course. Don't worry." I ruffle his hair so things won't seem so serious. "Everything will be just fine." We do a high five when we get to the school, and I watch him walk off to the entrance for the little kids. I know it's not true what I said to him. Things won't get better. They'll only get worse. I know it like you know some things. Things you see but just can't stop.

XIV

Lucien's there when I walk through the door. The world behind him fades to gray and suddenly he's all there is. He's leaning back against the wall, his uniform pants slouchy on his narrow hips. They don't look like that on anyone else. The collar's up on his navy blue shirt, and he's wearing his *grand-père*'s sweater with the swirly-whirly monogram and the spray of moth holes on the sleeves. His curls are hanging over his eyes and he's reading his book on Schiele. He doesn't look preppy somehow, uniform and all. When he sees me there, his eyes light up. He tosses back the springy curls, and the slenderest smile tips his lips. He'd grab me, I know, but people are milling all over the place, and Mrs. Dane, the principal, is standing at the door. Lucien lightly kisses my cheeks. Says my name and shows me a painting in the book. *Standing Woman in Green Shirt.* "She looks like you," he tells me, and I stare at her smudgy eyes.

In art class we get to be together again. That's where it all began for us—I mean, after he first smiled at me in front of the Michelangelo. We started to sit at adjacent desks and talk as we did our work. Lucien is much more talented than me, and I've learned a lot in just the few weeks I've known him. He draws really well—his grandfather was an artist—and has a style that's all his own. We're doing a project together now for what our teacher calls "public art." That just means stuff to display around the school. A lot of kids are doing landscapes of the grounds or the view of the river out the door. They're trying to "bring the outside in"—the outside to the inside—which was kind of my plan when I painted the vines on my bedroom wall. Now the whole idea seems dumb. Nobody thinks they're actual vines; they just think *How sweet, what a cute idea.* Ditto for the "outside-inside" art at school.

Up till now, Lucien and I have kept our project under wraps. Today, however, Mrs. Pasacalia wants to get a peek. We lay out all our drawings, making sure that no one else can see. Our project requires secrecy.

"Trompe l'oeil," says Lucien under his breath. (That's "trick the eye" in French.) "Each circle, you see, is a giant replica of circular objects in the world—a button from a jacket, a label on a fruit. This one here is the top of an ordinary screw."

"How interesting," Pasacalia says.

"We're going to place them all around. On the floors and streets—wherever we go."

"Very witty," she comments then. She looks at Lucien, not at me. She knows that it was his idea. Or maybe she's in love with him.

"It's like a game!" cries Lucien. "What will they think—*zee* people—when they see *zees* giant button here?" He's starting to get excited, which always makes him sound more French. "Perhaps they'll imagine a giant coat. And after that, a giant man who will wear *zee* coat. How *beeg eez zee* house *een vich ee leevs*?"

"It's brilliant," Pasacalia says. "A little like guerilla art. When are you going to install?" I know she feels cool saying words like "guerilla" and "install." She lets her hair fall forward as she leans a bit toward Lucien. He tells her we have to finish the group and paint them to look more real. We'll photocopy them after that—dozens, maybe hundreds—and place them everywhere we go. Not just in school, but all over Buenos Aires.

Lucien is all worked up and hyper, and I think it's cute when he's manic like this. His eyes get sort of glittery and he talks real fast and out of breath. I only wish he didn't tell Pasacalia so much. I liked it better when it was a secret between just us. I'm glad when she leaves and I have him to myself again. He's brought in a stack of old and faded postcards. To him they're not exotic. He found them at home in a cardboard box. I replicate the circular stampings on the back. The washed-out dates, the names of places I never knew existed anywhere in this world.

XV

At lunchtime Lucien and I go out to the grounds and sit behind a tree. It's chilly still, and I press into his sweater's warmth.

"How will I survive two weeks?" My words are a garbled against the wool.

"It is so unfair," he murmurs. "They force us to lie and then get angry when we do. My father was the same as yours. He would tell me not to leave the house. But I didn't obey. I would jump out the window and run away. I would go to *Grand-père* and stay with him."

Whenever he talks about *Grand-père*, Lucien starts to smile. His grandfather was an artist. One of his paintings is in a museum. But like his daughter after him, he was also a cultural attaché.

"When I went to *Grand-père* my father couldn't bring me back. *Maman* wouldn't even let him try, plus my father was afraid of him. Sometimes I'd stay away for weeks."

"It's nice that your mom stuck up for you. My mom used to be like that, but she's different now that Dad's around."

"It's bad when there are two parents," Lucien comments grimly. "You never know which side they'll take. You never feel secure."

"So you like that your parents are divorced?"

"There is no divorce. My parents are still married. They just prefer to live apart. When *Maman* gets angry, she threatens to send me back to him."

"Did she threaten to do that on Friday night?"

"Yes, she did. And I may have no parties now." He puts his lips to the top of my head. "But she's so busy she soon forgets. She goes away this weekend again, and would never know if I had one tiny party with only one special guest. That's why it is all so sad." *Triste,* he says. And I agree.

For a while we just sit there, our eyes gazing out across the grass to the Rio de la Plata and the blurry edge of sky. It's early spring here in the southern hemisphere, and several boats are sailing on the choppy waves. They're going fast, heeling over in the wind, their white sails bright with sun. The river looks silver, like its name.

For a few minutes I play with the idea of telling my mom I want to stay late to work on my art class project. But Mom's in a pretty ungiving mood. I turn to Lucien to speak, but he stops my words with the press of his mouth. Leaning back, eyes half closed, all I can see is the shape of his curls and a rim of green from the trees above. My eyes fall shut and I float away. Each kiss goes on forever, and I'm drifting in a deep green sky, spinning, weightless, like a leaf.

XVI

At home the atmosphere is very tense. Dinnertime is worst of all, everyone making small talk, pretending we get along. I try not to be a sullen brat. Sullenness, Bill warned me, would kill all chances of reprieve. But it's hard to be something else. So when Dad, in his oh-so-perky voice, starts asking about my day at school, I can't dredge up the words. I sit there, silent, like a stone. Dad moves on to Tyler then.

"A lady came to school today and taught us to write a poem."

"You mean to say there's a bard in our midst?"

"A what?"

"A bard. A poet. Let's hear the poem you wrote today." Dad looks around the table. "Shall we listen to the poem?"

"I'd love to hear it." That's from Mom. I think she's a little high on wine.

"Why not?" booms Bill, like everyone's deaf.

"Tessa?" prompts Dad.

"Yeah, fine." I'd rather hear anyone other than Dad. Tyler looks at each of us to see if we're for real.

"I might not remember all of it. I don't have the paper home with me."

"That's quite all right," says cheery Dad. "Just do the best you can." There's a moment of total silence. Then Tyler clears his throat.

"'The Dog,'" he says. "By Tyler James Bell.

"A dog is what I really need.
A dog to play and jump and feed.
He can be brown or black or white.
A gray dog is also all right.
I'll hold him tight
every night.
The end."

"Bravo!" says Dad.

Mom claps her hands. "That's lovely, Tyler," she says to him. "And yes, we're still thinking about that dog for you."

"Remember," says Dad, "having a dog is a big responsibility. You'd have to walk him twice a day. Even when it's raining. And we'd put you in charge of feeding him."

"I know, I know," groans Tyler. He's heard this speech a million times. "So when can we go and get him, Dad?"

That occupies us for a while, everyone talking about different dogs. Beagles. Pugs. Alsatian hounds. Then that runs out, and Dad asks Mom what she did today.

"Nothing much," she answers. She sort of sounds like me.

"No meetings? No lunch? No tennis balls?"

"I skipped the AIMA meeting," she says. That's a women's club to which she belongs. They go to lunch and take excursions and things like that.

"Skipped on account of other plans?"

Mom looks pissed—at me *and* Dad. "I think you know there were other plans." She pointedly tips her head toward me. Like that's more polite than saying out loud that I ruined her day.

"Oh, right," says Dad, as if he's forgotten all about my grounding, though I know he hasn't. He'd never forget. Mom shoots us both a fed-up look that says we're totally wrecking her life, she can't even go to lunch. The tension grows, which makes me feel better in a way. I want them to feel the fallout. Especially my traitor mom.

"Maybe," says Dad when she still looks pissed, "we can set up a system of telephone calls. And you can get back to your normal routine."

"Don't worry," I snap. "You can go to back to your 'normal routine.' Playing tennis and doing your nails. Maybe Dad can get a tracking device." I feel Bill's irritation first. He's rooting for me, but I just can't manage to play the game. Dad comes next.

"We can make it three weeks if you want," he says. It's like he has a script. My mom's enraged by the comment about her life.

"Tomorrow I work at the Casa," she says. Her voice is low but menacing, and I feel like a cornered mouse. The "Casa" is Casa de Ronald McDonald, a residence for children with cancer, where once a week she and some other women volunteer. They do arts and crafts with the mothers to keep them occupied while their kids are at the hospital. "I think you should come along with me. It just might help your attitude."

The entire family's staring now. Of course, Mom's won, and everyone knows it. She's gotten her revenge for my remark (if she were so totally into herself, would she volunteer in a home for dying children?) and tomorrow she gets to live her life. I can't say no to her big idea or I'll look like a heartless jerk.

"That's a splendid idea," my dad concurs.

"Glad you approve," she says to him. Her voice is like a spike. No one asks Bill about his day, and it's really quiet after that. He'll be glad to get back to his job in Guatemala. I bet he can't wait till Friday night. Tyler looks sad and stricken. He's probably thinking about his dog. The one he'd hold tight. Every night. The end.

XVII

There's another email in my box. The subject reads: "I Know Something's Wrong. Just Talk to Me Tess." That makes two I haven't read. My mood can't really get any worse, so finally I open them. The second one first. It's probably less full of hope.

Come on, Tess. Where are you? I'd worry, but I know from Norah that you're all right. That's all she'd say, so there has to be more. I don't want to say it either, but I'm starting to think there's another guy. I wouldn't blame him, whoever he is. I'd fall for you too if you came walking into my life. Of course, I hope there isn't. But I still have to know the truth. So do me a favor, Tessa. If it's really over, tell me up-front. Don't leave me here waiting like an asshole. Think of it as a good-bye gift. I promise I won't be mad at you.

Mike

P.S. Even if you have ten new boyfriends, I'll still love you. I mean it.

I know he means it. That's just Mike. The guy you'd call if you lost your keys. If you needed a dollar or someone to say you looked all right. I met him at school in computer lab. I was just about to throw a book right into the screen when he suddenly came between it and me.

"Wow," he said. "Remind me not to get you mad." The slightest emphasis on *you*. He asked what I was trying to do and gave me some useful tips. After that he helped me with some research I was doing for my art history class. He was clueless when it came to art, but he was funny, and I knew right away he was really smart. I never went for dumb guys, beautiful or not.

For our first date, Mike took me to the National Portrait Gallery in DC and then to some bistro type of place where we talked about the all faces we'd seen and which Thomas Jefferson portrait was best. He looked at the details, not the strokes and arrangement of parts. But it was fun how he'd notice every little thing. He said he'd never really thought about art until he'd looked at it with me. Yet I couldn't get him to understand any nonobjective art. "Looks kinda like a boomerang," he'd say about a yellow shape, or "Is that supposed to be a face?" I used to find it funny, but now I can't imagine being with someone who sees art like that. As smart as he is, Mike will never understand the things that Lucien understands. Lucien's an artist. He looks at the world in a different way. When he looks at a painting, color is color and form is form. There's no story or meaning attached to it. He sees the world on the picture plane. And now, it's strange. I'm starting to see the way he sees. I'm starting to see the world as flat.

XVIII

Dear Mike,

I'm so sorry for not writing sooner. I felt so bad and kept putting
it off. But you're right. There is a guy. Which, apparently, you
figured out. It was probably crazy of us (u and me) to think
we could have a relationship from 6,000 miles away. All
the same I never thought this would happen. You were the
greatest boyfriend anyone could have, and I know for a fact
there are dozens of girls who'll be happy to hear that you're
available again, and I hope (and know) that you'll find one soon
(probably next week) who will love you the way you deserve
to be loved. Like I said, I'm sorry, but I just have to follow my
heart in this. Please try to understand. I will never forget you.

Thanks for everything.

Love,
Tess

XIX

I t will be nice," says Lucien when I tell him about going to the cancer place. But instead of doing arts and crafts, he says the mothers should draw and paint.

Two years ago his grandfather died of cancer. For several months, he was in some special hospital and Lucien visited every day. All they ever did was draw. They drew the patients sitting in the sunroom and the strange equipment everywhere—the special chairs and cold machines, the tubes and trays and *objets d'art* from that special world. They sketched the man in the nearby bed. Recorded his face as it slowly changed and he finally died. "It was sad but it was also nice. You'll see," he says. "You'll like it, Tess."

So here we are at the Casa. The volunteers take turns bringing in the projects, and Hela is in charge today. She's an older English woman whose husband works with BP. She has pinkish hair and a kindergarten-teacher voice. "You have a choice," she explains in her singsong Spanish to the moms around the table in the big communal dining room. She unveils the project: fun-foam hats to give to their kids. They can make a dragon or a shark. The dragons are more colorful, but the sharks have cooler teeth. Both have plastic googly eyes that wiggle when they move.

It's not as easy as you'd think. The patterns are hard to follow and the glue gun's kind of dangerous. The women are very focused, intent as they cut and fold the shapes. Sometimes they speak, asking one another what step comes next. They laugh whenever they screw things up, and Mom or Hela or this other woman, Netta, tries to help them out. Mom's Spanish isn't all that great, but she knows the words they need to hear, like "seam" and "score" and "inside out." She's a stranger to me. I wonder where she learned those words or how to make these hats.

At five o'clock some kids come back from the hospital escorted by an aide. They fall onto the couches not far from the tables where we sit. They're quiet and limp, and mostly just stare at the TV. Some are wearing paper masks—to keep out all the germs, I guess. Another mother joins us at the table. She's pretty and young and everyone says hello to her and puts on the hats to show her the project of the day. She parks her stroller and borrows someone's dragon hat. Putting it on, she dances for her baby. Makes funny faces and dragon noise. The baby's huge and bloated and attached to some murmuring machine. She does all sorts of things, hat on, hat off, but the baby never smiles. She tells the others to put on their hats, and takes a picture of them all. I snap one on my iPhone too, all the moms in their fierce sharks and bright dragons. I wonder how they manage to say *"Queso!"* and plaster on a smile.

When it's all over, we fetch the car from the parking lot. Mom drove today, and Hela sits in front with her. I sit in the back, staring out the window. It's hard to shake the aura of the afternoon. Not that I really want to. Like Lucien said, it was sort of nice. Sad, but nice. And peaceful. I think about drawing that woman's bloated baby. It was like a Christ Child in a painting by Parmigianino, a lump on the Madonna's lap. I realize I don't even know if the baby is a boy or girl.

I wish I could talk to Lucien. Tell him how it went today. How right he was when he said that I would like it. How maybe I'll go back again. As I'm thinking about Lucien, we pass the American Embassy. It's after five, so people are coming out of the gates and heading for their cars. It doesn't look like an embassy; it looks like barracks, stolid and gray behind its long, flat barricade. My dad drives to work in his own car, so of course, we don't stop to pick him up.

We drop Hela off at her house in the San Vicente suburb. Even her house looks English. There are flowerboxes everywhere and the hedges are sculpted into shapes. When she gets out, my mom suggests that I move up front, that she feels like a chauffeur with me in back. We drive for a while and then she asks, "Want to stop for something to eat? Dad won't be home till late tonight."

"Yeah. Okay."

"Kansas?" she prompts. That's a popular restaurant near our house. Not too fancy. I like it there. You can tell by the name what the food is like. Most of the time I've been here with the family. I've never come with Mom alone. Which means, I guess, she has something to say.

XX

It's pretty early for dinner in Buenos Aires, but a lot of foreigners like this place so it's fairly crowded even now. We wave across the restaurant at my mom's favorite human being, Cathy Blaine, and her perky mother, Sandy. I can't believe she doesn't invite them to sit with us.

"I need a glass of wine," she says.

So do I. My life's more stressful than hers these days, and it doesn't seem fair that I'm not allowed to have a drink to just take off the edge. Sometimes I think of popping one of my stockpiled pills. But the truth of it is, I'm not sure which is which. I probably ought to ask Lucien.

"I'll give you a sip," Mom offers, as if she's read my thoughts. She has no idea that I drink wine every weekend now. I avoid her eyes and look out the window onto the tree-lined parking lot. The glass is slightly tinted, so the late-day sun looks like moonlight on the ground.

"What did you think of the afternoon?" she asks me after a little while.

"It was interesting," I tell her.

"Come on, Tess. You know that's not an answer."

"I thought those hats were really dumb. What are they going to do with them?"

"Hela's projects are always strange. But when Carla came in and put one on and tried to cheer up the baby, well, I started to see it differently."

"But it didn't cheer the baby up."

"Maybe not then. And maybe it won't. But it made Consuela happy to see her dragon put to use. And everyone smiled for Carla to take the photograph. Just a few little laughs can be very good in a place like that."

"Is her baby going to die?" I ask. I realize as I say it that this is what's been on my mind, casting the small black shadow there. My mom doesn't answer right away. Her wine arrives, and she passes it over for me to sip. I take a gulp and slide it back.

"No one knows," she answers. "Carla believes she's going to live. And everyone hopes along with her."

"How can she be so cheerful? I don't understand how—"

"I don't either," my mom replies. "And I know this might sound selfish, but it's part of why I work there. I want to learn what those women have. Where they get their hope and faith."

There's nothing I can say to that, and we sit for a while sharing the wine. Our food arrives. American food—hamburgers and fat french fries—which I'm somehow in the mood for. I'm very hungry, though I'm not sure why.

"It makes me think," my mom picks up as we start to eat, "about all the nonsense in our lives. All the unimportant things that seem so consequential, but really don't mean a thing." I swallow. Gulp. She's going somewhere with this, I know. *"Un vino más,"* she says to the waitress whizzing by. I don't say a word. "We're so lucky, Tessa. Our family, I mean. We're healthy and well. There's nothing we need or want. We ought to be so grateful. So grateful and happy every day. When I go to that house and see those mothers living with that daily pain, well, I feel *ashamed* that we aren't happier than we are. Does that make any sense to you?"

"I guess," I say. I'm wary. I don't really think she's talking about *my* happiness, but I'm sort of surprised she's talking about this stuff at all—especially to me.

"Your father's been under pressure, Tess, so things are a little stressful now." My mind snaps back to their whispers the other morning and how she looked when I went downstairs. "The move was a lot of work," she says, "and then getting the office under way. There are so many open cases, too. And unresolved things from the previous legal attaché. " She pauses for a sip of wine. "And then, of course, there's Jerry—Jer."

"What about Jer?"

"Well, Jer's a bit of a problem, Tess."

"What do you mean?"

"Apparently he's having a little trouble adjusting to the job."

"Weird," I say. "I thought he was really into it."

"A little *too* into it," Mom replies. "Apparently he's been tracking leads, starting investigations, without consulting with your dad. He still has the missionary zeal."

"That's funny," I say.

"Not really, Tess. The FBI has no jurisdiction overseas. They're only here to cooperate with the local law-enforcement groups. You can't spin off on your own like that."

"Sorry, Mom. I still think it's kind of funny. Jerry getting all gung ho."

Mom cracks a smile.

"In any event, on top of all his other tasks, your father has to rein him in. He'd also like him to give up his gun while he's in Buenos Aires. It's Jerry's decision in the end, but Dad just thinks it's a good idea."

"Dad should let him keep it. Sooner or later he'll shoot his own foot." Now Mom's smiling all the way, almost laughing really, as she slides the glass of wine toward me.

"There's a party," she says in a suddenly much lighter tone, "on Friday night at that wonderful house where they lodge the marines. It's for people your age—kids of embassy personnel as well as guests from the other embassies in town. I know your father's grounded you, but I think he might let you go to this. The marines will be your chaperones. You've met a few at Chatter Night, so we wouldn't have any worries there. I think it really might be fun. Tess, you know," she adds in an almost pleading voice, "I really want you to have fun. I want you to enjoy this time."

I could argue with that. Tell her how, if this were true, she would leave me alone and let me run my social life. But I sense it's not the moment. We're having a sort-of decent time, and she's basically ungrounding me, at least for Friday night. Already I'm fabricating plans. How to make this work for me. I'll go to the party for a while. Show my face, then slip away. We'll set a place and Lucien will meet me there.

So I tell her all right. The lame-ass party might be fun. I don't say "lame ass," naturally. And I try to sound somewhat grateful as I reach for another swig of wine.

XXI

I tell Lucien the good news: I am ungrounded for Friday night. His face lights up and he shakes back his curls. I tell him about the party and the plan I've made for sneaking out. I think he'll be excited, but instead he says, "I want to go to the party too."

"It's at the Marine House, Lucien—"

"That's why I want to go. I've never been to a party like that."

"But people will see us. Americans. And my dad might hear—"

"That's why it's exciting. And think of it, Tess, we can start our circle project there."

"I really don't think—"

"I'll get an invitation."

"How?"

"My mother is important. She just has to make a call. She knows everybody everywhere. She's friends with your ambassador." He gives me something like a wink. "I'll be there, Tess. I'll be at your party Friday night."

❧

Later on, Lucien and I meet in the art room during our free period. We're making a map for where we'll place our circles. We've photocopied hundreds of the plate-size seals, dozens and dozens of each design. The next part will be harder: setting them out without being seen. We thought of enlisting Esme's help, but she's so brain-dead half the time and we never know when she'll be at school.

"So tell me," Lucien says again, putting two more circles on the map. "I want to hear about yesterday."

"It was just like you said. Nice but sad. I felt like I'd entered another world."

"You did," he says. "The land of the sick. I remember *Grand-père* calling it that when he was in the hospital. They have different customs, he used to say. A different language and different rules. 'You do not want a passport here.'"

I take out my phone and search for the photo of the mothers in their hats. He leans in close to look at it.

"It's a wonderful picture, Tess," he says. "When you know where it is and who these laughing people are, well, it suddenly means something else. Something the photograph doesn't show."

I turn off the phone and go back to arranging the circle groups. A breath of air tickles my neck, lifting the wisps of hair. It touches again, and I realize it isn't air at all. Lucien's fingers are tracing my neck. They're skimming lightly over my jaw. And now they're drifting toward my ear. My ear is like a seashell, and one delicate probing finger is circling its way inside.

We lie down on the art room floor behind the shelves crammed with paint and brushes and tall white tubs of glue. It's a warm and sheltered nook. One of the walls is formed by rolls of paper standing upright in a box. At the other end are some big, tall puppets of papier-mâché left by last year's senior class. I feel like they are guarding us, these red-cheeked women, these gauchos with their long black braids. The air is tinged with turpentine and the smell of drying clay.

"I want to make love to you," Lucien whispers in my ear. "This is our place. Doesn't it feel like our place to you?"

"We can't," I say. It's hard to speak. He is kissing my bones the way he does, shoulder to shoulder along that ridge. And now he's gliding downward, and I feel his mouth parting the opening of my shirt, nibbling the edge of bra.

"What if—" I'm wondering what bra I wore and at the same time picturing Pasacalia's face, the face she'd have if she came in the room and found us here. I open my eyes to the glare of daylight overhead. Everything is crystal clear—the speckled ceiling, the paper fence, all the glue jars upside down. His hand is on my hip bone. Then under my bunched-up skirt. His fingers thread in and start to descend. They are gentle, but not so gentle now. It's startling as he touches me in that tiny red spot between the flesh. He holds me closer, pressing his body against my hips. His hardness feels tense and urgent, straining against his pants. He takes my hand. Pushes it to the zipper. He wants me, needs me, to pull it down. But my fingers can't seem to hold the tab, that metal tongue at the very top. I gasp with pain as he grabs my wrist. It feels like a little bone has snapped.

XXII

OMG. R u crazy, Tess? Have u absolutely lost your mind? In school? R u kidding? What if someone had found u there? I can't even stand to THINK of it. I know you're in l—e, but please stop being crazy. And STOP feeling guilty—that's even worse. I can't believe he used that "if you love me" line.

BTW, Mike told me that you ended things. He was sad, of course, but he said he knew. I felt so bad—he's really sweet. Guys like M don't grow on trees.

Anyway, Tess, be careful. Love makes people crazy, and you're making me very scared.

Love 4ever,
Noreeeee

P.S. Don't worry, I dumped your email and blacked out my history.

XXIII

Lucien's forgiven me. At first I didn't think he would. I figured he would just break up. I wouldn't blame him if he had. Everyone knows how it is with guys. I mean, once you start, you sort of have to finish it. You can't lead them on, then suddenly decide, *Oh no!* It's much too strong for stopping. He couldn't help how he grabbed my wrist. He didn't mean to hurt me. There's hardly a bruise. Just a small blue dot that looks like a flower.

XXIV

Old Bill comes to visit in my room. He plops himself down in my plushy chair with the green and purple pillows. Looks out the window into the night.

"It's nice here," he says. "It's cool what you've done." He's leaving for Guatemala on Friday afternoon. He's already got his buzz cut, like he's going off to war. He won't be back till Christmas, if the Volunteers let him off.

"Figured I ought to fix it up," I answer after a little while. "Since I'm going to spend my life in here." I turn from the computer and look across the room at him. He's so simple and straight. He's never wished for anything that hasn't been in his grasp.

"It doesn't have to be like that," he tells me in a quiet voice.

"Like what?" I say, though I know what he means.

"Like the way it is. Like this. Everything used to be okay. I don't understand what's happened to you."

"To me?"

"Yeah, you. You've really changed."

"I haven't changed. I'm exactly who I always was."

"So what do you mean—none of us knew who the hell you were?"

"Listen, Bill, if you want to talk about serious change, take a look at Mom."

"What about Mom?"

"Are you kidding me, Bill? Her friends wouldn't even know her if they passed her on the street." I can't believe just how much Bill doesn't see.

"Yeah. So what? She's having some fun. Is there anything wrong with that?"

"It's fine for Mom to have some fun. But not to be a traitor—"

"*What?*"

"When Dad was away, things were fine. We all were pretty happy, weren't we? Nobody fought and Mom never grounded anyone. Everyone just lived their life."

"So you're saying everything's all Dad's fault?"

"I'm saying that he's out of touch. He doesn't realize we're not the kids he left behind when he went away. He can't come back and jump right in like nothing's changed."

"I haven't changed," Bill answers. Which strikes me as funny, but also sad.

"You and Dad are the only ones."

"What is that supposed to mean?"

"It means we've *evolved* since Dad's been gone. Mom's been running everything—but not like in some dictatorship. We talked about stuff—she acted like I was an adult. Now she gives up all her power and lets Dad be in total charge. You were away at college, so maybe it's not so clear to you."

"I don't know what you're talking about."

"I know you don't. So, what do you want? I mean, what do you actually want to say?" I soften my voice as I ask the question at the end. Bill just wants things to be all right. He's like Tyler that way. But Tyler, of course, is nine years old.

"I just want to help," he answers. "I see you making every-thing worse. Saying stupid stuff. Acting snotty with Mom and Dad. Can't you just play the game sometimes?"

"Not when they try to run my life—tell me who can be my friend, where I can go, what I can do. They even think they can get in my heart and tell me who to love." Bill gets a little squirmy.

"Yeah," he says, "I heard that you broke up with Mike."

"You *heard*? How?"

"I heard it from Mike."

"Mike?"

"Yeah, Mike. He emailed me."

"I didn't know the two of you were so close."

"I always liked Mike. All of us do. I hope," he adds, seem-ing even more uncomfortable, "that this other guy—this French guy you sneak around with—is worth the trouble he's going to cause. I really hope you don't end up regretting things. Like dumping Mike and whatever else you're planning to do."

I'm pretty shocked that dumb old Bill knows I'm still seeing Lucien. I want to know how he knows it too—or maybe I really don't.

"Listen, Bill"—I try to sound firm—"I told him as nicely as I could. He's a really good guy; I just can't help the way I feel."

Bill looks sort of unconvinced, but he doesn't know what to say. I'm sure he's never been in love. Not even with Melissa Thorpe, who he dated all through high school and who dumped him just before the prom. Maybe that explains why he's so obsessed with Mike and me.

"Just try to be smart. I won't be around to tell you when you're screwing up."

"Yeah," I say. "I'll try not to be an idiot." I look at his face, adding in a gentler voice, "I wish you didn't you have to go."

"Yeah, me too. But anyway, Tess, I'm gonna keep in touch with you. You and Tyler both." He gets up from the chair and stands there looking serious. He must have found a used big brother manual and read to chapter two. At the doorway he stops and turns around.

"You know," he says in a philosophical-sounding voice, as if he's been thinking way-deep thoughts, "it wouldn't be hard to screw up your entire life."

XXV

Thursday night. Dad's brought Jer for dinner. Apparently he forgot to notify my mom. She's in the kitchen with Nidia, who was just about to leave. Neither of them looks too thrilled. Nidia's pretty gifted, though, and whips up some extra food real fast. As usual, I'm sent out to the living room with a tray of Triscuit canapés. Good old Jer is sitting there, buttons open down his chest, hair and chains all sticking out. He and dad are drinking Scotch, talking about al-Qaeda or something Very Serious. Bill's with them too, pretending to be a colleague. They all stop talking as I come in. Like the conversation's CLASSIFIED.

"Hey, there, Tess," Dad practically sings as he takes a napkin and a snack.

"Hello, Tessa," Jerry says. Before he can ask what's "actually" in the canapés, I quickly tell him manchego cheese and peppers, not a speck of mushrooms anywhere.

"Thanks," he says, and goes for two. "Anaphylactic shock's no joke." Thanks for the information, Jer.

All during dinner he talks about the bygone days when he ran his mission in the Bronx. Tyler's rapt as he tells about the Bloods, the Crips, and the Latin Kings, and all the kids he saved from a horrible life of crime. He dressed in white to avoid the colors of the gangs, and even guys at Rikers had heard about Brother J. Dad remarks that Jer was "sure a legend," and the jerk doesn't even realize that Dad is making fun of him.

During dessert we find out that tomorrow morning dad has to fly to Asunción. That's in Paraguay, which is part of the territory the FBI in Argentina is responsible for. Jerry's going to stay in town and "mind the home fires" for the week. My brain starts to race when I hear this news. My dad away for one whole week. Right away I'm thinking of Mom. She shows some signs of softening; she's letting me out of my grounding to go to the party Friday, right? Yet glancing around the candlesticks, I don't feel all that hopeful; her face looks anything but soft.

"You just found out?" she asks my dad, as if no one else is there.

"Yes," he says. He might as well have said "shut up." His voice is just that clipped and flat. I guess he doesn't want it known that he has to answer to his wife in front of the legendary Jer. I suddenly feel very protective of my mom and I really hate my dad. I have this fleeting fantasy that his plane will crash over Iguazú Falls and fish will gobble him for lunch.

I look across the table and, of course, there's Tyler looking upset. I can't stand seeing him all stressed out, and I mention something to break the ice—something I read about Paraguay.

How people think the "triple frontier"—Brazil, Argentina, Paraguay—is a haven for Arab terrorists. That sets Jer off on some big discussion of Ciudad del Este and the "porous" border where the countries meet. He must say "porous" a dozen times. He loves the word "porous," I don't know why. But it eases the tension—at least for now—between my mom and Dad.

After that, Jer and Dad start talking about some embassy stuff. Jer assures Dad that while he's away, he'll also "keep an eye" on us. Do you know how safe that makes me feel? By now my mom looks almost sick.

Finally dinner's over, and Jer and Dad go into the "den" for another Scotch and a cigar. On my way upstairs I pass the two of them smoking away. Jer's legs are crossed, and I see the gun on the ankle where his pants ride up, black on his purple argyle sock. Dad, it seems, still hasn't made any headway there.

Before going to bed, Dad comes in to say good-bye. He'll be leaving tomorrow before I'm up. His visit really wrecks my mood. I was thinking full-speed about Friday night and how to fix it with Lucien. Dad tells me that my mom has told him about the Marine House party, and that he's decided to let me go. He acts like Mr. Wonderful, giving me a gift. He tells me he loves me and wants me to be happy and he'll see me in a week. I don't even know what I actually say. Maybe I tell him "Have a safe trip." Maybe I say "I love you too." Because that's the script. That's what I have always said.

XXVI

The Marine House is a big, sprawling place in Vicente López. I was here once before, when we first arrived. The grounds have a pool and tennis courts ringed with tall green trees. Inside, however, it looks kind of like a frat house. Only neat, of course, because the guys who live here are marines. They probably have inspections. Bounce dimes off the beds and stuff like that. My mom stops the car in front of the gate.

"Look, isn't that Cathy Blaine?" she cries. She honks her horn and waves at Cathy's mom. She's so weird and excited. It's like I'm six on the first day of school. "It's going to be great," she says. "Hey, look at that guy at the door—good God! I never had chaperones like that."

There's a big, muscled marine standing at the entranceway. He's not in an actual uniform—though the polo shirt and khakis practically qualify as one—and I have to admit, he looks like he'd take care of things. He nods as Cathy shows ID, then heads on in, her ponytail like a trail of yellow smoke.

My mom looks at me through the car's blue air. "Tess," she says, "can't you just be happy? When I was your age, my biggest thrill was the Halloween hayride down to the lake. Can't you see what a wonderful moment this is for you? Can't you see that you have to grab it while it's here—like the ring on the carousel?" I stare at her. She must know how totally weird she sounds. She stops for a minute. Shakes her head. Then, turning toward the house again: "When it's over, Tess, you'll wish you had."

Mom, of course, has had a rough day. My dad took off for Paraguay, and who knows how it was with him—if they patched things up before he left. She was the one who drove Bill to the airport. All by herself, which must have been tough. He'll probably come for Christmas, but it's still a great big deal to her. I think she's afraid he'll get some horrible disease, typhoid fever or something like that, working in the wilderness.

Bill and I said our good-byes before I took off for school. The usual stuff. Have fun in Guatemala. Don't drink the water. Drop a line. We hugged in a sort of awkward way. He used to hug great when I was small, but I guess he forgot or maybe my standards were not so high. "Remember what I said," he said in the middle of that stiff-armed hug. "Use your head. Don't screw things up. *Adios*. I'll be in touch."

Anyway, tonight Mom's going out with friends. Maybe that's the reason she's all so weird and hyper. Maybe she's glad that Dad's away too. She can be the way she used to be. Do whatever she wants to do. Tap perfume just behind her ear. Go out to dinner dressed in jeans. She checks the rearview mirror. I see her as she drives away, tossing her hair with a movement that looks young and free. A peal of laughter rings from the house. I turn toward the sound and—*click*, like that—forget about Mom.

XXVII

There's a blur of people inside the house. I see kids from school and others I don't recognize. Most of them are American. There's music playing. It's very loud. The marines sort of look like college guys—well, beefed-up, clean-cut college guys—but not like someone's parents, and they're friendly and talking to all the guests. The nice one, Carlos, says hi to me and tells me to have fun.

In the central room there's a table of food and coolers filled with sodas. There are couches all around the place and a huge TV stuck up on the wall tuned to a grassy soccer game. Guys in yellow and guys in red chase the two-toned ball. Esme's here, which I can't believe. I beeline across the room to her, glad to see someone I'm friendly with.

"Hey, Tessa, love! I came with Wid." I'm sure she means love like "l-u-v," but the way she hugs me I know she's glad to see me too. There are faint blue circles under her eyes, but aside from that she looks really good in a tight little skirt and a fluttery blouse.

"Is Lucien here?" I ask her.

"Who cares about him? Check out these militia blokes." She blows a kiss at two marines standing against a wall. The "militia blokes" *are* kind of cute. A few look even younger than Bill. But if Esme thinks they'll be breaking any rules for her, she's going to have to think again. They're the best of the boys. The Eagle Scouts. They go by the book or they'd never have landed a post like this. By day they guard the embassy, checking badges, scouting around. By night they live in a mansion of a frat house. Why would they want to mess that up?

There's a giant pool room down the hall, Esme quickly lets me know. We head in that direction, past great big rooms with hardly any furniture. It seems so strange—six young guys living in this giant house. "Want to smoke a joint?" asks Esme. "There's no wine or beer or anything."

"We can't smoke here. Are you out of your mind?"

"There's a garden out back. I know where to go."

"Esme!"

"Really, it's totally safe. I've already had a toke out there."

It's stupid, I know, but I don't resist as she takes my hand, leads me to the kitchen, and out a swinging door. The sounds of the party echo as we slink along the path. We end up near the tennis courts. There's a wall of bamboo, and overhead, the thick black trees. I take a drag of Esme's joint. I already feel high just breathing the air of the cool spring night. We're in the deep grass in the spiderwebbed hibiscus bush behind the birds of paradise. It's dark, delicious, and dangerous.

XXVIII

When we go back in, everything is soft and hazed. I say hello to Cathy Blaine. Tell her I really like her shirt. The shirt seems to glow. There's a fuzzy aura around its edge.

Canadian Alice is actually here. "Your boyfriend's cheap," she tells me. "Love's like war, and all is fair."

"You didn't help," I answer, and she shrugs like it's irrelevant that her scam didn't work and she got me grounded for two whole weeks. Esme and I go into the room where the pool table is. There's another TV, and on the screen the same frenetic soccer game.

"Marvy," says Esme, her English accent thick. "I'm daft in the head for billiards." A couple of guys are playing, and she sidles up to watch them shoot. The guy whose turn it is stops and aims a smile at her.

"Are you good luck or bad?" I'm surprised by his voice; he's American. Tall and dark, he somehow looks more European. Tight black jeans. A boatneck shirt, like something Lucien might wear. I know he doesn't go to our school.

"I'm whatever you want," says Esme. She's great with stupid lines like that. She ought to write a book.

The other guys laugh, and the cute one says, "I want you to be good for me." I watch as he plays, planning his moves, measuring with the wooden cue. When he leans near the table to take his shot, the muscles ripple in his arms. There's another flutter down his back. He wins the game, and Esme coos, "So how'd I do?"

"Good," he says, and smiles again.

"I'm Esme. And this is Tess." He looks at me. Volleys another smile.

"Hi," I say.

"My name is Paul. Can I get you some drinks?"

"What kind of drinks?" says Esme.

"Nothing too exciting. Though if you're good—if you're really good—we might just manage to fix them up. It isn't easy. These guys are hawks." He glances at a big marine. "Coke all right?"

"I'd rather some orange Fanta." That's crazy Esme, of course, not me.

When Paul comes back, we sit on a couch. There are other people lounging around. Cathy Blaine is one of them, and Greg Muldoon, whose mom's with Immigration. Maureen's there too, and a couple of guys from Canada. "You embassy people too?" asks Paul passing us the drinks. Esme says no; she's here with her dad who works for the Britworth Company. I'm sure she just made up that name. He looks at me.

"Embassy," I tell him. "You?"

"I'm here on a break," he answers. "Playing polo for a while." Esme turns and rolls her eyes. But then he adds, in a way that makes you think it's true, "It's my grandfather's graduation gift. One year off to play with the best."

"Hell," says Greg, "can I rent your grandpa for a year?"

"Yeah," says Paul. "Old Jake is cool. He still plays polo a bit himself back in Illinois."

"Illinois?" coos Cathy. "Who'd ever think they play polo *there*?" She fiddles with her ponytail. It's long and thick. She's a natural honey-colored blonde. I'm not quite sure if Paul's for real. But I have to admit he's cute. He's also splashed something into our drinks. And no one noticed. Not one of the hawks. I'm floating on a soft, dark cloud. Then suddenly in the light-filled doorway, there he is. There's Lucien.

XXIX

My entire body goes into a spin. I forget about polo-playing Paul and the fact that he's spiked our drinks with gin. My heart dislodges and springs to my throat. I can actually feel it beating there.

"Lucien, you're finally here!" I wrap my arms around him. He's lean and kind of bony, not at all like Paul or the superbuff marines. But I like how he feels; he's what I want.

"Tess, *ma belle*," he whispers. And then he murmurs, "Who's that guy?"

"What guy?" I'm sort of talking into his chest.

"The one that you were smiling at."

"I wasn't smiling!"

"Yes, you were. I was watching from the door."

I pull away to look at him. "Don't be crazy, Lucien."

"But you were."

"So what? People smile all the time. Plus, I wasn't smiling like—"

"You were smiling your pretty smile. Your *beau sourire*. Don't you think I know your smiles?" He himself isn't smiling at all, and I realize he is serious.

"Lucien, stop. If I was smiling—well, the smile wasn't meant for him."

"What is Esme doing here?"

"She came with Wid." I take a breath. "No matter who I smiled at, you're the one I want to see."

"Really?"

"Yes."

"I'm sorry, Tess. I'm a jealous cat. I want for us to be alone."

"Me too," I say. He seems to have forgotten that I'd wanted to go somewhere else, but that he'd insisted on coming here. "Have a taste," I whisper. He doesn't reach to take the cup, so I hold it up for him to sip as if he's a little child.

"Mmm," he says. "You're a very bad girl."

We go floating around, sharing the drink. Lucien has brought some circles along with him, and so we begin our project here. As we sit on a couch I bend as if to scratch my leg, and I set a circle on the floor. We go room to room and no one sees us doing it. We find the kitchen and put one there. Two on the floor of the dining room. Giant buttons. Chiquita banana, edged in red. The circles look good; they're funny. But Lucien doesn't smile.

We wander through the cool and empty places. Wind our way down a quiet hall. There's a flight of stairs leading up to the dark. We look at each other but do not speak. He's been quiet since he got here. Since he caught me in my *beau sourire*. He starts to go up, but I pull him back. There are probably only bedrooms there. He gives me a look that breaks my heart. A look that says he doesn't think I love him. There's a door beneath the stairway, and he opens it up and peers inside.

A long brown string trails up to a light. It's a strange little room for storage. The walls are slanted like the stairs. The room is full of sleeping bags. He draws me inside. Picks one up of the coiled bags. Hardly moving, he closes the door. The light's too bright and dangerous, so he pulls the cord and turns on his phone. A patch of blue in the sudden dark.

He slips the tie and the bag unrolls. As I sink to the floor, I notice the words US MARINES stamped across the orange plush. Lucien tastes like gin and pot. He takes off his shirt, and I smell the silk beneath his arms. I love that smell; it's Lucien's, but I'm scared of it now in the blue-tinged black. His breath is quick and shallow as he lowers down on top of me. I'm really high, yet I'm wide awake. His heart is beating very fast. Whose heart beats faster, I don't know. But mine is in my throat again. It's pounding there as he kisses me and his tongue slips in my mouth.

He is moving now. Teeth on my dress, pulling it down the way he does. The startling warmth and wetness as his mouth takes in my nipples, pursing them in his lips. When I open my eyes, there's nothing to see. There's only the dark and the eerie blue light. I'm here but not, it's the strangest thing. It's like I'm not inside myself.

Lucien is moving down, sinking south to the hem of my dress. My big rose dress. My Georgia O'Keeffe. Slipping off my panties. How cold and bare. How hot and wet.

This time I draw the zipper down. I have to, I know; I can't run away from him again. It makes me shiver, that part of him I'm holding. The way it overflows my hand.

"I should put something on," he whispers. For a moment I don't know what he means. He moves and fumbles. Takes something from a crinkly pack. Then kicks off his pants and the thin, stretchy underwear. More fumbling with the condom. It isn't romantic, this fumbling part, and for just a second I think I can't. Then, *"Belle,"* he whispers into my hair, and I swallow the fear and part my legs. He has to know I love him now.

He strains against my wetness, pushing harder with every thrust. Then something gives way and I hear my own voice, like a startled bird. Like one of those birds who lives in reeds. Deeper and faster he pushes now, so frantic and so desperate, he's like someone I don't know. It's like he's in pain, and the pain won't stop. But then it does. It suddenly, abruptly does, and he lets out a gasp and tumbles down on top of me, all wet curls and hot, damp skin. Everything is limp and still.

XXX

I t's midnight when my mom arrives. I climb into the car, terrified she'll somehow know. But she's in her own world, all
chatty and bright. I wonder if she's okay to drive. "That's
Esme, isn't it?" she asks as my friend heads toward a waiting car.

"Yeah," I say. "I didn't know she'd be here." We watch her
slide in, skirt riding up on her gangly thighs.

"Jerry was there?" she asks me next.

"Jerry who?"

"*Our* Jerry. Jer. Isn't that him in the doorway there?" I spin
around, and sure enough Jer is coming out of the house. Shirt
half-opened down the front. Carrying his shoulder bag. In his
hand he's holding one of the circles we put on the floor.

"What the hell's he doing here?" The words come blurting
out of my mouth. I'm completely freaked to know that he was
in the house.

"You know Jer. Probably 'checking up on things.' And don't
say 'hell,' it isn't nice."

Oh my God. I can't believe he was skulking around and I

didn't even see him there. And he has a *circle* in his hand! Mom just shrugs. "I guess he has nothing else to do." Right away she forgets about Jer, and the whole barrage of questions starts. How was the party? Who was there? Did I meet anybody interesting? I try my best to be chatty back. Tell her about the pool room. The polo-playing Paul. My high's worn off and I feel so weird. My underwear is soggy, and it hurts when the car goes over a bump. I feel so changed—so different—I can't believe she doesn't know. That it isn't screaming out at her.

She tells me about her evening then. It's so much easier when she talks; it takes a lot of effort to make my voice sound normal, like nothing is going on. They had dinner in a lounge-type restaurant nearby. She and the girls—"the usual crew." Though tonight there was someone new along—a military wife named Anne McDermott. Seven kids, can you believe, and refuses to have a maid. One of the boys is Tyler's age. Maybe they can meet, she says. Tyler could use a nice new friend.

On and on, she rambles, and her voice is like a hum. With every passing second I sink more deeply into myself. I'm freaked enough just feeling the funny way I feel, but thinking of Jer— knowing he was in the house while we were in the closet—well, it almost makes me sick. I tell myself that he just popped by. At the very end, for the quickest peek. Inside my head, so much stuff is going on. I don't have the space to think of Jer. I put him away in another place. A special little Jerry box in a corner of my brain.

Mom talks on, and I gaze out the window as we pass all the

familiar sights. I'm so mixed up and I can't put a name on the way I feel. Yet something's creeping over me. I feel it like a shadow, like a cloud drifting in from far away. It's not exactly sorrow. It's more like an ache, an all-over twinge like longing. Like when something's over, some part of your life, or when someone you love has gone away and is never coming back again.

XXXI

I go to church on Sunday. Eat *medialunas* in the sun as I amble through the breakfast room. I say hello to Cathy Blaine. Ask if she liked the party.

"I thought it was nice," she tells me. And then a little nervously: "What did you think of Paul?"

"I thought he was cute."

"I wonder who invited him."

"I don't know. Maybe he crashed."

"The marines wouldn't let a crasher in."

I think of Jer and wonder. "Maybe he's friends with one of them." And then I ask, while we're sort of on the topic: "Did you see that creepy older guy? The bald guy with the open shirt?" Cathy gives me the weirdest look.

"Doesn't he work with your dad?" she asks. I can't believe she knows this. And I'm sick to hear that she saw him too.

"I thought it was Jer," I murmur. "But what the hell was he doing there?"

"My mom says he's watching out for drugs. Keeping an eye

on the embassy kids." She finishes her cruller. "I'm surprised they didn't kick Esme out. I think that girl is always stoned." Across the room I see that my mom is watching us, thinking, praying, I might start hanging out with her. "So you really don't know what Paul's about?" Both of us are scouting for information that the other one doesn't have.

"No," I say, "but I'll ask around. By the way, what time was it when Jer arrived?"

"How should I know?" Cathy says. She's sidling away from me, eyes on Maureen. I don't understand why my mom thinks she's so wonderful.

I walk to a corner and check my phone. I've checked it at least a hundred times.

Since Friday night I haven't heard from Lucien.

That afternoon I hang with Tyler, looking at dog adoption websites. He seems to like the ugly dogs, the frazzled fur, the mismatched ears.

"How was the party?" he asks me while we're sitting there.

"You would have liked it a lot," I say. "There were big TVs and couches. Potato chips and soda, plus all the marines you know were there."

"I like Carlos best."

"Me too." The telephone near the computer rings. Mom's gone out, so I answer it.

"Tessa?"

"Yes?"

"It's Jerry here."

Something catches in my throat. Like I've had a little seizure there.

"Tessa?"

"Yes?" We're like echoes in an empty room.

"Just checking in," he tells me. "Everything copasetic there?" I think of the Marine House, but my mind can't finish the sickening thought.

"We're fine," I manage to say to him.

"Your mom at home?"

"No."

"Is Tyler there?"

"He's somewhere." Beside me, my little brother scrunches his face as if to ask who's on the phone. I put a finger to my lips. I don't want Jer to talk to him. It's none of his business where Tyler is.

"A-okay," says Jerry. "Just want to make sure that everyone's accounted for while your dad is out of town." Here's the part where Mom would tell him thanks a lot, but there's no way I will say those words.

"We're fine," I answer. I'm not really rude, but I'm certainly not friendly. And Jerry finally says good-bye.

The phone is shaking in my hand, and I quickly put it down. For the thousandth time I tell myself that Jer didn't see me with Lucien. That if he had, I would have heard it in his voice. I *would have*, I assure myself. I'd know; I'd know; I'd somehow know.

Tyler, meanwhile, finds another must-have dog. This one's

really hideous. It looks like something for cleaning pots. Flora is the poor mutt's name.

"I'd call her Smoky," Tyler says. The dog is reddish with bristly hair; it has no resemblance to smoke. Tyler loves her from afar. I know how he feels. There's an ache inside. And nothing will make it go away.

Back in my room I dump the pill stash out of my purse. I think the OxyContin's blue, but I'm not sure what the others are. One is round and tiny. So small it can't be very strong. I swallow it down and go to bed.

XXXII

B y Monday I'm a total wreck. Lucien hasn't called me yet. Not even his usual *Bonjour* text. All my longing has turned to dread. I'm terrified of seeing him, of reading in his damp brown eyes that he doesn't love me anymore. Maybe it's even worse than that. Maybe he actually hates me now. Hates that we did the thing we did and can never go back to the way we were. I almost can't breathe as we near the school. Tyler takes off with one of his friends and I reach the door alone.

Lucien's standing outside instead of in the lobby, and I think, *Oh God, he wants to talk to me alone, he's going to break up with me.* With a jolt I see that he's cut his hair. Sort of, I mean. It's long and short, as if he hacked it off himself. He looks so unfamiliar, and I want to turn and run.

My mind flips back to Friday night. I did it for him. To make up for that time on the art room floor. He was so remote at the party that night, and I wanted to bring him back to me. Remembering now, I know it didn't bring him back. If anything, it made him more unreachable. I think about the very end, how lost in himself he seemed to get, almost as if I weren't there. A dip of panic takes my breath. I should have said no. It's all my fault. Everything is over now. I'm going to run. I'm ditching school.

But suddenly Lucien lifts his face. He sees me and his eyes get soft. I know that I'm not dreaming this. He closes the book and comes to me, rushing across the space. From somewhere in back, he pulls a rose. A dark red rose, whose petals crush as he draws me close.

"Tess, *ma belle*. I missed you." He kisses my hair and the curl of my ear. "Are you all right? I need to know that you're all right."

And suddenly I think I am. I don't even care that he's hacked his hair in the craziest way, and he looks all strange and slanted and not the way he looked before.

XXXIII

Turns out, he went to Mendoza with Solange. Rushing out for the early flight, he'd left his cell phone in his room, which is why I hadn't heard from him. They spent the day in the provincial capital, where his mother had meetings, and after that they traveled to a friend's remote *estancia*.

"I can't believe you couldn't have reached me somehow!" I know that I sound needy, but that's what I am. I'm needy. I need to know that he understands how abandoned I'd felt when he disappeared without a word.

"There was no privacy," he says. "There were people everywhere all the time. And out at the *estancia,* they have a rule—no cell phones. *Maman* had to put hers in a box." With his fingertips he tilts my chin. We're sitting outside in our usual place beneath the tree. "I'm so sorry, Tess. I didn't know you'd be so—" He cuts himself off as if to reconsider the words. Then: "Don't you believe I love you? That I love you no matter where I am?"

"I don't know!" I blurt at him. "I didn't know why you disappeared, and it made me so afraid. Especially after—" My words break off and I search for a way to say it. I realize I can't. I don't know what to call it, what we did that night beneath the stairs. Lucien is smiling now. It's a crooked, gentle kind of smile. Like the way I smile at Tyler when he's innocent and cute.

"You little puritan," he says. "You little sweet American. Do you actually think that because we had sex I love you less?" There it is. He's said it. It was nothing for him to form the words. He's shaking his head and the smile is fading from his face. He looks at me intently, his dark eyes very still. "I thought of it all week-end long. On the plane to Mendoza, I thought of it. I thought of your skin and your soft little breasts. I thought of pushing into you and how warm and tight you were inside. Lying in bed with the sound of the wind, I thought of it a thousand times. How could you think—how could it even cross your mind—that after that I'd love you less?"

"Because I didn't hear from you. Please," I whisper, "don't disappear like that again."

He draws me into the narrow circle of his arm. Presses his mouth against my hair. "Mendoza's very beautiful. The land goes on forever. It's pale and green, and the shadows are purple in the slopes—"

"Don't disappear like that again."

"It drizzled all day. We rode on horses through the hills. The sun came out and the colors changed. And then it began to rain again. The sky was black like it had a bruise, and it made the snow on the tops of the *cordillera* look very, very white."

"Lucien." My voice is not a murmur now. "Don't disappear

like that again." He loosens his grasp around my arm and draws away to look at me. His gaze is so intense and still that I almost have to turn from it. His pupils are enormous. There's only a narrow rim of brown.

For several seconds he doesn't speak. Then he says in the softest voice, "I won't disappear like that again." He leans in close to kiss my mouth.

For a while we just sit like that, pressed against our tree. Then: "Tess," he says, "I want you to come to my house with me. I want you to spend the night." I smile at that and shift a little in his arms. "*Maman* is traveling this week. The apartment is all mine."

"Lucien—"

"I'm serious. This time we will do it right. We will have dinner and drink some lovely wine. And afterward I'll take you to my bedroom." He puts a finger to my lips. "It won't be like the first time, Tess. It will be sweet, more beautiful. This time I'll make love to you. This time it will be for you." I kiss the finger against my mouth.

"It sounds so beautiful, Lucien."

"Then say you will."

"How can I? I'm grounded for another week."

"But this is the week my mother is in Paraguay."

"My father's there too—"

"Your father's away?" He eases back to look at me. "You didn't tell me your father was gone! This is the perfect moment, then."

"Except that I have a mother, too."

"But your mother can be worked upon. She let you go to the party, *oui*?"

"That was special, a one-time thing."

"Tessa, *belle*, I need you to come and stay with me. I want to make love in the proper way."

For a moment I imagine it. I close my eyes and see it all. I am in the red apartment, walking along the wall of glass. It's a starry night and the room is lit with candles that twinkle in a hundred jars. I'm thinking of lies as I walk along the edge of sky. One beautiful lie that I can tell, because now that I've imagined it, making love, falling asleep in Lucien's arms—I have to make the dream come true.

XXXIV

I go with my mom to the Casa de Ronald McDonald again. I don't do it for her: I want to go. I like the moms and I like the supportive atmosphere. In a funny way it makes me think of Girl Scout camp—the big communal dining room, the chore charts hanging on the wall, and the tables all sponged and clean.

It's quiet when we arrive, and Hela tells me why. "There's a rose today," she whispers, indicating a vase on a shelf beside the door. "That means one of the children has died." For a second my mom just closes her eyes. It looks like the rose Lucien brought to school for me.

There's an unwritten rule that people don't talk about anyone's case, and no one mentions the death as we sit at the table and Netta displays the dragonfly brooches we're going to make. There are seven mothers here today, including cheery Carla, who's very skilled with beads. I feel like a klutz beside her. My fingers seem enormous as I grasp the little specks of glass and struggle to thread the wires. Carla's so fast that she makes two, each in a different color scheme. She pins one on the stroller where her giant, gasping baby sits, still attached to the humming machine. Today I learn the baby's name—Liliana. The brooches are really pretty. I put mine on. I plan to wear it every day—on my shirt or jeans or the backpack that I use for school.

On the drive back home, after we've dropped off Hela, my mom announces that I'm not grounded anymore. Just like that. And stranger still, she tells me to keep it between "just us"—meaning her and me, and not my dad. I want to hug her, I really do, but she's driving the car and I don't want to die before my night with Lucien, so all I say is "Thanks."

Then she goes on. "I talked to Jerry yesterday." My fabulous mood takes a little dive. The creepy guy's been calling every single day. "He says he knows where the drugs have been coming from at your school. It's the Dutch boy, Wid, and several of the local boys."

"How does he know?" I ask her.

"He didn't say, but he told me he's on a mission now to keep an eye on the embassy kids. Sort of one-man youth patrol."

"Don't you think that's a little weird?"

"It might be odd, but he means well, Tess. He wants to do something to make his mark." She shoots me a curious sideways glance. "I thought you'd be glad to hear that your French boy isn't on the list. By the way, Jer says his mother's lovely. She's the cultural attaché to France." A heartbeat pause and then she adds, "Though I guess you'd know that, wouldn't you?" I give her a look as if to say *duh*, and she almost cracks a smile. "Maybe," she says in the same light voice, "when Dad comes home we can have a talk. Maybe we could meet the boy—I mean, if you still want to see him." I'm very confused. It's hard to read my mom these days. First she ungrounds me behind Dad's back, and then a second later wants to involve him in my life.

"We could plan a dinner," she goes on. Her eyes are straight ahead again, so I can't read anything from them. "With the boy and his mother. What do you think?"

"Yeah, okay," I tell her. "Am I really not grounded anymore?"

"It's over," she says. "Just please don't lie to us again."

"I won't," I say in my steadiest voice. Though, of course, I already have.

XXXV

Here's the plan. On Friday night Esme and Kai will stay at my house, and on Saturday night we'll stay at Kai's. That's the story, anyway. My mom won't suspect if we do it this way; sometimes we take turns like that. Luckily she knows Kai's mom, who also belongs to AIMA, so automatically Kai's okay.

So we plan this girlie sleepover thing, and after school on Friday, Nidia, my mom, and I make a bunch of stuff to eat. We even bake trays of cookies like we sometimes used to do back home.

It's sort of fun hanging in the kitchen, fooling around and trying to talk in Spanish. Tyler's there too, licking the bowls and scavenging for chocolate chips.

Funny thing is, my mom takes off almost as soon as my friends arrive. All dressed up in her brand-new jeans and high-heel boots, dangling car keys in her hand. "Your mum is hot," says Esme once she's out the door. "I never knew your mum was hot."

Tyler's upset. Apparently he and Mom had plans to watch a movie, but she totally forgot. We let him hang out with us for a while. Esme thinks he's "precious" and keeps asking if she can bring him home. Like I'd ever let him in that house. Then she decides to paint his toes, each a different shade. At ten or so the telephone rings. Tyler runs to grab it, hoping that it's Dad. I don't even ask when he comes back.

"It was Jer," he says, plunking down on the bed.

"What'd he want?"

Tyler shrugs. "He wants to know that everything's copa-septic."

Kai gives a hoot at how he pronounces the Jer-like word. Her English vocabulary's huge.

"What'd you tell him?"

"Everything's fine and we're having fun."

"Did you tell him what we're doing? Does he know Mom's out? Does he know that we have company?"

"I guess," says Tyler slowly. "I told him some of your friends were here."

"Listen, Ty, don't tell him anything anymore. It's none of his business what we do."

"Mom doesn't care. She says he's checking up on us while Dad is out of town."

"All the same, don't talk to him. We can take care of ourselves just fine." He stares at his multicolored toes. He doesn't care that weird little Jerry spies on us. He's having the world's best time right now, playing the pampered prince.

When Tyler finally goes to bed, I tell my friends to be on the watch for a small, neurotic-looking guy with a hairy chest and a slick bald head. Esme says, "Cool," like it's some kind of game. To me it isn't funny. All night long I have the sense that he's watching the house. That he's off in the dark behind a hedge, staring at our windows through a small pair of binoculars. I'm glad my room doesn't face the street.

I try to put Jerry out of my mind. I tell Esme and Kai what my mother said—that she's open to meeting Lucien.

"Are you sure you want that?" Kai inquires.

"What do you mean?"

"Well, you really don't want her knowing too much." I shoot her a look, and she explains. "Too much about Lucien, I mean."

Esme chimes in. "Sometimes he's a crazy boy."

"Lucien isn't crazy." I think it's kind of funny that Esme should say a thing like that when she's the most psycho one of all. Only someone really dented would hang around with Gash.

"Fine," says Kai. "Don't say I didn't warn you, though." She shrugs her shoulders. "So what's the plan? Is he going to meet your father, too?"

"My mom suggested dinner—"

"Including Solange?"

"Well, yeah, of course."

"It's settled, then. Especially if your dad is there. I told you about my father. He met her once at some event. It was all he talked about for days. If Solange wants your father to like her son, I promise you he will."

"It's because she's French," says Esme. "And has all those gorgeous shoes." She stretches her legs and looks at her feet. "These are hers. They couldn't be mine. Hey there, Tess, have you got any wine?"

"Are you crazy?" says Kai. "Her parents would know if we drank their wine."

"I'll run out and get some, then. Unless you want some pot."

"Do you want to land us in major shit?"

"All right, all right. I'll get some wine."

"Maybe vodka's better. It doesn't smell on your breath," says Kai.

"Watch if you're being followed," I warn as she pulls out her phone.

"I'll make the driver zigzag," she says in a deadly serious tone. She calls a *remise* and grabs her purse. When she comes back she swears she wasn't followed; she made the driver do tricky things—pull into a lot and turn around, go backward down a one-way street.

We drink the vodka with lemonade and start to do our fingernails. Esme gets up to dance around. She dances like a girl from the 1970s, rolling her hips and swinging her hair from side to side. Gash must have taught her to dance like that.

They're going to Venice at Christmastime, she tells us as she sways around. She and Gash and Evangeline. After seeing his creepy cowboy boots, I can't even stand to think of Gash.

Never mind to think of the things she does with him. I mean, if they actually do those things, which maybe, let's hope, they don't. Kai can't believe that Esme would go on a trip with him accompanied by Evangeline.

"It'll be fun," says Esme, flipping her hair like a go-go girl. "She can be my mum. We're staying on the Grand Canal. Hotel Danieli. It's superposh."

"You're gross," says Kai. And Esme says yeah, but she's never been to Venice and wants to ride a gondola. She's getting drunk, starting to bump into things.

Four a.m. and my mom's not home.

XXXVI

We haven't been here by ourselves since the day that Lucien sketched my dad. And Esme was there for most of the time, so that sort of doesn't count. It's so quiet and still. The wall of windows that holds the sky is a glowing lilac-blue. The glow seeps through and tints the artwork on the walls. It settles like dust on all of Solange's treasures, the Russian icons, mysterious jade, the dancing lovers from Côte d'Ivoire. The lights of the city are coming on. They twinkle and tangle in the trees ranged along the balcony in their massive Incan pots. Lucien has lighted the Moorish lanterns, and dozens of candles glow like jewels throughout the room. There is music playing faintly—Andean flutes and hectic drums—and I feel like I am floating as down below Buenos Aires pulses, glittering in the dusk.

We sit on the couch, where, weeks ago, Esme was strewn, her jumble of pills scattered about. Everything was crazy then, but now it's all serene. The top of the table is made of glass and encased underneath are silver things I never really saw before—

keys and knobs and tiny statues of Hindu gods. A tall white orchid blooms on stilts in a china pot.

Lucien opens a bottle of wine. They brought it from Mendoza. Rich and red, delicious wine, and we drink from deep, huge goblets that fill with its heady smell.

I am wearing a long green shirt. I am trying to look like the girl in Schiele's painting. I got it from Mitra before she broke away from us (her boyfriend doesn't like Lucien; he's *peligroso*, so he says) in exchange for a pair of jeans. She bought it in Milan; it's silk. On the collar, I've pinned my dragonfly.

"You're beautiful, Tess," says Lucien. "I love that green against your skin."

I look at my wrists and the space of arm beneath the sleeves. I know it's true, I'm beautiful, if Lucien sees it with his eyes. I'm beautiful and happy. No, not happy, it's more than that. I'm something miles and miles beyond—a feeling that has no words for it.

We sip our wine. There's a drop of purple on his lip, and I lean to his mouth to lick it off. We kiss for a long time, stretched out on the white alpaca couch. Darkness comes leaking into the room, and when we get up, it is half past ten.

"Let's cook," he says, and we amble to the kitchen, our glasses almost drained. We don't really cook. We take out the food the maid has left and heat it in a pan. It isn't French; it's some kind of spicy Peruvian shrimp.

I set the table in a corner of the long red room. Lucien tells me where everything is. The silver in the felt-lined drawer. The hand-turned plates with their chartreuse glaze. The napkins as huge as blankets for a baby, of purple Shantung silk. I light the tall black candles. There's another orchid in a pot. It's willow-green and looks like a moth hovering in the blurry air.

For fun, we sit very far apart. I'm at one end and he's at the other, miles away. It's very sexy to eat like that. I want to touch him, but I can't. We talk about things we've never spoken about before.

"What is like not to be the only child?" It's Lucien, of course, who asks.

"It's nice, I guess," I tell him. I really don't know since I've never been the only one. "I can't imagine not having a brother on either side."

"Which one do you like better?"

"I like them the same."

"How can you?"

"I don't know, but that's how it is." I sip some wine. I can't explain. "Do you wish you had a sibling?"

"I wish," he says, "there was someone else. Maybe a brilliant sister who would please my father and make him less concerned with me."

"Is your father so concerned with you?"

"Yes, *mais oui*. He bothers me all the time."

"What can he do? He's so far away."

"He comes in my dreams and talks to me. 'You waste my time.' 'You ruined my life.' Sometimes he says he wishes I had not been born."

"You dream these things?"

"But they are true. It's because of me that he left Solange."

"What do you mean?"

"I caused distress between them." Lucien stirs. "When *Grand-père* died I got very wild. I was so enraged that he was gone. I was thirteen years old and I felt I'd lost my only friend."

"I've never lost anyone close to me. . . ." I pause for just a moment. Then, "What sort of wildness, Lucien?"

"I started to deface things."

"What?" I stare past the candles at his face. His cheeks look hollow in the dark, all the light caught on the ridge of bone above.

"I became a vandal. A Visigoth. I started to destroy things."

"What kind of things?"

"Beautiful things. Things that other people had made. I scrawled on statues. I shattered glass. Broke mosaics in the park. Sometimes I set things on fire."

I try not to move as I draw a breath. Talking seems too dangerous; yet the silence is thick, a menace too. I find my voice. "I understand." The words travel out, down the table's gleaming length. I know they're not true. But I wish they were. There's a slow, faint chill lifting the hairs along my neck.

For a while Lucien doesn't speak. And then he says in a raspy voice: "It felt like something I had to do—end things, smash things, burn things up." He lets out a breath. "So that's the way it happened. I put my anger everywhere. And one day they arrested me. My parents fought about what to do. My father wanted to send me to a boarding school. My mother wouldn't hear of it. So my father moved out, and soon after that *Maman* was posted here."

"Your father left by choice."

"But if not for me—"

"I don't believe that, Lucien." I grope around to find the words. "We're all responsible for ourselves. And adults most definitely are because they can do whatever they want. Your father moved out—*you* didn't. You shouldn't blame yourself."

"*Maman* says that," says Lucien. "She thinks he's weak, and secretly she likes when I defy him. I can see it in her face."

"It doesn't sound like your mother respects him very much. Do you think she loves him anymore?"

Lucien ponders this a while. "She loves him and then she hates him. I think she would like a stronger man. Someone like *Grand-père*."

A silence lingers after that. Thoughts of my parents run through my head. How hot and cold they are these days, and how sometimes I feel their tensions are due to me. But I don't want to think about that right now. I chase the thoughts, and will myself back to where I am. Never before has Lucien told me things like this, and while part of his story frightens me, I want to know all there is to know. On his lips there's the hint of a trembling smile. The slightest tilt at the shadowy edge. The candles flicker in his eyes.

"Come here, Tessa. Come to me."

XXXVII

We go into his room. I amble around and look at the artwork on the walls. The brilliant orange painting, its edges running to earthy red. The Schiele-inspired drawings of skinny men and pointy twigs. A series of collages made with torn *Le Figaro*s. There's the mirror, too, with the spidery cracks, which I now know for certain he has made. And that window with the fractured X. He goes to a chest and opens a drawer. "I never show these to anyone." Under some scarves, the drawer is filled with sketchbooks—dozens and dozens of dog-eared books.

"Sit," he says, and he plumps the pillows high against the headboard so they form a plushy mound. He takes out maybe fifteen books and climbs aboard the bed with me. "This is from four years ago." He points at pencil-scribbled date. "I used to go sketching with *Grand-père*. Sometimes we'd go to his country place. I have lots of drawings of sheep and cows. But this one is from Paris."

I look at the page he shows to me. A woman walking a tiny

dog. Her dress is spotted, frilled at the hem, and the dog has pointy ears. *5 Mai* is scrawled on the pavement under her feet. Next is a sketch of a skinny boy; he leans on a lamppost to talk on his phone. There's a sexy girl on a motorbike. Furry skirt and tall black boots. She makes me think of Esme, this unknown girl from *5 Mai*. Another sketch shows items on a table—glasses, keys, a menu with a long, frayed cord.

"And here's my brioche," laughs Lucien, pointing at a fat, round shape on the circle of a plate. On the following page is a drawing of an older man smoking a curvy pipe. Like French people in a storybook, he is wearing a beret. I know it's *Grand-père* before he even tells me, and I feel as if I know him and I love him as if I do.

Lucien shows me older books. He jumps from the bed to bring them. Excited now, he drops them into a growing pile. We sit together, legs curled up. I see drawings he did at six years old. Chairs and cats and bowls of fish. A boy on a horse and a woman in a window behind a scrim of lace. Even back then he could draw so well. I love the portraits of *Grand-père*. In one of them he is wearing a robe with a poppy print and on his feet are great big slippers that curl at the toes. Lucien laughs. "He brought them from Morocco. Whenever I went to visit him, I always put them on."

Lucien seems so happy as he looks at the pictures from long ago. *"Maman!"* he cries as we come upon some painted works. Her lips are the brightest shade of red and match her pill-shaped purse. Her name is scrawled around the edge—*Solange,*

Solange—the *S* like the swirl of a long green snake. Even as a child he knew that she was beautiful. That she had a flair, a kind of flame, that people could not resist.

The drawings change as Lucien gets older. He shows them to me in order. I feel as if I'm traveling through his life with him, seeing not just the places and people he knew, but *him* as well— how he saw the world, what caught his eye. He was interested in the simplest things—a cast-off shoe, ivy on an iron gate, an onion, a shell, someone's shirt turned inside out. I remember what he said that day when he sketched my dad. He said that drawings were more intense than photographs. I think it's true. Photographs are distant. They are filtered through the camera lens. Lucien's drawings are seen through the eye with nothing in between. He decides how he will save the moment, what he will show and what he will hide. His fat brioche is not like any photograph. Its underside is shaded with delicate, loving strokes, and the top is rounded like a cheek. I can almost taste its sweet, rich core.

We come to a book that's bound in reams of ribbon. It looks like it's been mummified, but Lucien unwinds the ribbons and opens it for me to see. He's very good at portraits now. *Grand-père* is gaunt; the hollows in his face are dark. His hands are large and prominent and sit on his lap like agitated animals, the fingers knotted in and out. His poppy robe has been replaced with a hospital gown, strings at the neck falling, tangled, down his chest. There's a picture of his gnarly feet, the second toe much taller than the rest of them. A basket of fruit that someone sent with a folded card. There are drawings of other patients. Women sleeping in their chairs. Men in bathrobes playing cards. A nurse with an empty-looking gaze.

Toward the back of the book are Lucien's *Studies of the Dying Man*. Page after page of the man who slept in the nearby bed. The changes are so subtle, yet when you look back from the last to the first, the difference is a shock. I want to go back to the happier books, but I wait till Lucien is done. I wait till the end, to the very last drawing in the book: a still life of a paper cup.

"He died," says Lucien quietly. Then he takes the long blue ribbon and winds it back around the book. "I never showed anyone," he says.

I draw him close, and he lowers and sinks against me, his arms around my waist. His breath is shallow, the way I breathe when I've cried a lot and only fatigue has made me stop. I hold him very gently, the way you'd hold a child. After a while the rhythm of his breath slows down. I feel the heaviness in his limbs and I know he's gone to sleep.

XXXVIII

When I wake in the middle of the night, Lucien's head is resting on my stomach and my hands are tangled in his hair. His books are poking into my legs, and I wonder how we fell asleep. I don't want to move and wake him, so I stare beyond the edge of bed at the orange painting on the wall. There's still a flame in one of the candles we brought to the room, and it makes the entire painting glow like a fog of color in the air.

He stirs on my lap. "Tessa," he says, in a whispery voice as if just remembering I am here. I can feel the contours of his lips as he kisses my stomach through the shirt. He opens the buttons slowly, silent as a ritual. The air is cool as he parts the cloth, and I feel his eyes like the tip of a brush pulling across my skin. The gaze of his eyes is almost as real as the touch of his mouth as he kisses the dent beneath my throat, the blue in the space between my breasts, the hollow at my hip.

It is not at all like the night in the closet under the stairs. It is gentle and very tender and Lucien says he loves me. Again and again he whispers the words. When he comes inside, it is different too. He is very slow and careful, as if listening to my heart. He covers me with his silky heat, and the dampness on my skin grows hot. We move in a rising rhythm that takes on a force that is all its own—until something bursts at the center of our bodies, something I feel as liquid stars.

We stay together, not wanting to part. Lucien clings, his fingers splayed on the top of my arms. I think of him setting things on fire. Shattering, cracking, breaking things—and I want so much to keep him safe so he'll never do things like that again. The candle flickers in its jar. It's very low and nearly spent. I wonder if it's possible to save a person from himself. Everything's so fragile, and flames go out in a wisp of air. Dreams dissolve when you open your eyes.

XXXIX

My dad is strange when he returns from Paraguay. First of all, he comes straight to the house instead of stopping at the office, which he never does. It isn't even five o'clock. He sends Nidia home and announces that he's taking us to dinner. Mom seems pleased, but very surprised. It's lucky she's even home herself. She's just breezed in from the hair salon.

Tyler's thrilled that Dad is back. He gets all dressed up and wears his funny mink bow tie. My grandma Anne, my mom's mom, made it from an old fur stole, and Tyler thinks it's beautiful. It's the closest thing he has to a dog.

Before we go out, Dad brings us to the living room to give us some gifts he bought for us in Paraguay. Crocheted shawls for me and Mom. Hers is white and mine is black. He's also bought Mom linens—embroidered napkins, a beautiful snowy tablecloth, which I know she'd never use back home because of the ironing entailed. "Thank you, darling." She kisses his cheek. I guess she has forgiven him for being so mean the night before he left.

"And now for Tyler," says my dad. Tyler's been chomping at the bit, watching us open up our gifts. Breathless, he takes the bag from Dad. He draws out the gift and stares at it. It looks like a traveling jewelry box, pale tan leather embossed with designs.

"Open it," Dad tells him, and when he does there's a belt inside. Except that it isn't really a belt. It's a collar and a leash.

Tyler's mouth drops open. His eyes get round, and I think for a minute he's going to faint.

"It's for your dog," Dad tells him. "We'll pick one out this week."

Tyler still can't close his mouth. It's as if he's afraid to draw a breath. As if he thinks the leash and the collar will disappear if he takes a sip of air. I touch his shoulder to jostle him, and he topples sideways into my lap. My parents laugh.

I look at my mom. Her hair is pale with highlights and her eyes are especially blue and bright. She's wearing the shawl Dad gave her, holding it clasped right over her heart.

We go to a restaurant near our house. It's pretty fancy, actually, and most of the time my parents come here by themselves. When we first arrive my dad spots Carlos in the bar near the entranceway. Carlos is the nice marine. He waves to us, and Dad pops in to say hello to him and his date. The girl is pretty. She's Argentine. She has long black hair and sexy eyes, and she looks so right with Carlos, who's very dark and smooth tonight.

We sit at our white-clothed table. There are candles and a bowl of flowers. They're ginger flowers, candy-red, and they grow in the garden out back. The garden is lit with torches; I can see it from our table, and it looks like an enchanted world—snaky trees, plants with dark, enormous leaves like big black hearts against the sky. I'm feeling pretty mellow and getting into the mood of things when Mom's eyes veer across the room.

"Jim," she says in the softest voice. "I spy your assistant over there." All of us turn and look across the tables, through the motes of candlelight, to the faraway corner where they sit: Jerry and his mom.

"We should say hello," my mom suggests. So we all get up—it's protocol—and weave across the room.

"Jerry!" says Dad in a robust voice. We're all in tow like a bunch of ducks. Jer leaps up and shakes Dad's hand. Everybody greets Jer's mom. She says hello, gazing up from her glass of wine. She's soft like a little dough ball, and I understand where Jerry got his button nose. Her eyes are bright and sparkly. You can tell she loves being out with Jer.

Back at our table, we order drinks. "He really kept an eye on us," Mom remarks with half a smile. "Called us every day."

"Good," says Dad. "Keep him busy and out of things not his concern."

"So tell us," Mom interrupts him, "about your trip to Paraguay." She's doing double duty, both flirting and trying to placate Dad.

"He has to realize," Dad goes on, "that he's part of a team—and on that team, he's low man on the totem pole."

"Was the weather nice in Paraguay?" It's clear that Mom's not giving up.

Her voice is soft, solicitous—like Dad's not Dad and she's out on a date. She sips some wine and smiles over the top of her glass; a little red reflection dances on her chin.

"I don't want to bore you with that," says Dad. "Let's talk about Tyler's dog instead." Tyler leaps in, ecstatic.

"I already know which one I want! I saw her online. She's really cute. Tessa, tell him how cute she is."

"She's cute," I say. "She's really cute. We better get her right away."

"Tomorrow!" cries Tyler breathlessly.

"Where is she?" asks Dad, and we talk for a while about how we'll manage to pick her up. Like a broken record, Dad goes back to the list of things Tyler will have to do each day—feed her, walk her, and all the rest.

"Yeah, yeah, yeah," says Tyler, and at last Dad agrees that yes, all right, he'll call in the morning to check things out. After that, Tyler's in another world and can hardly even eat.

Mom, on her second glass of wine, mentions the Marine Ball. It's an annual embassy event, which I know she's been thinking about a lot. More than once I've heard her on the telephone discussing it with Sandy Blaine. I try to recall the last time I saw Mom in a gown. Dad's thinking the same, but about himself: "Tell me, Nan. When did I last put on a tux?"

"You might need a new one, Jim," she says.

"It'll still fit," he tells her, as if he's very proud of that. "And those monkey suits never really go out of style."

"I, however, am going to have to get a gown."

"Of course you will."

"I'm thinking I might have it made. Sandy says she knows some shops. With the dollar exchange, it really doesn't cost so much."

"Whatever you like," Dad tells her. And then he adds, "I know that you'll be beautiful no matter where you get your dress."

I glance at Mom. Can she actually be blushing? She dips to her glass for a sip of wine, then draws the shawl from Paraguay lightly around her shoulders, which are tanned and especially smooth tonight. My eyes move around the table. Tyler, in his mink bow tie, is busily dreaming about his dog. Mom is happy. And Dad and I are not at war. Yet Dad is weird, I can't say why. It's just been a week since I saw him last, but he doesn't look the same to me. I keep glancing across the table trying to pinpoint what it is. And then I think that maybe it's me. That I'm the one who's changed, not him.

XL

Lucien is going to disappear again. But this time he's let me know. Solange has to take a trip to Rome and asked him to go along with her. He'll be out of school for almost two weeks. I'm so jealous I could die.

On the Wednesday before he leaves, we go to the MALBA museum to see a special showing—an artist named Gallardo, whom Lucien really likes. After that we sit outside on the steps of the museum. It's bright and yet it's chilly. The sky reflects on the high glass walls, and the hard-edged glare makes something in my bones feel cold.

"How many did you do?" he asks.

I look at the circles I still have left. "Two on the floor of the ladies' room. One on the stairs and one near the Botero."

"You're such a guerilla," he says to me. "Next week," he adds, "you should put some in the embassy."

"It won't feel right doing it without you here."

"Tessa, no. It keeps us together, don't you see? I've packed many circles to bring to Rome. You'll be doing it here; I'll be doing it there. We'll be connected across the world." We sit for a while. I'm cold in just my sweater and I pull out my new black shawl.

"Pretty," he says. He slides in close. Gently helps me put it on.

"It's a gift from my dad from Paraguay. He brought home gifts for everyone."

"*Maman* went to Paraguay," he says. "But she didn't bring me anything."

"Instead she's taking you to Rome."

"True," he says, and starts to play with the fringe of the shawl. Then: "What will you do while I am gone—aside from putting circles down?"

"Nothing at all. I'll sit and mope."

"Will you?"

"Yes."

"You won't go to any parties?"

"No."

"And you won't do things with Esme? You know that Esme's very bad."

"I won't do anything very bad."

"And you won't go out with Kai and Wid to those seedy tango bars they like?"

"I won't go to any seedy bars."

"And you won't see that American?"

"What American?"

"The one at the party. The one you liked."

"I don't like anyone but you."

"I think he's following you around."

"What?"

"I saw him—twice. I know I did."

"Where?"

"Like a shadow, slipping away."

"You're making it up. You know it."

"Well, maybe it was someone else. Someone who's in love with you."

"What did he look like?"

"I don't know."

"You see—you're lying. You're making it up." Lucien smiles, but it isn't a smile with any warmth. He continues to toy with the length of fringe.

"I don't like to leave you alone," he says. "I'm so afraid that someone else will steal you off."

"Then why do you go away so much?" I'm smiling too, but the question is real. Shouldn't *I* be the one who's jealous here?

"Do you want me not to go?" he asks. And of course I know the answer.

"I want you to go wherever you want. I'd go too, if I were you. I just need you to stay in touch with me and not disappear the way you did when you went to Mendoza with your mom."

"I promise, Tess," he answers. His face is serious, slightly sad, as softly he repeats the pledge: "I'll never disappear again." He draws me close in the crook of his arm. "You must also promise, Tess, that you won't disappear from me."

"Lucien—" I start to talk, but he pulls me tight against him, so tight that all my words get stuck.

"I need you, Tess," he whispers. "You don't even know. You have no idea."

"Lucien, I need you, too—"

"I need you in a different way. I need you so I can stay . . . intact."

"Don't say that, Lucien. You're—"

"It's only because of you."

"Me?"

"Yes, you. You keep me good. I haven't done anything—"

"That isn't true." I try to make my voice sound light. I try to make a joke of it. "You cut your hair. You totally massacred your hair." Lucien doesn't even smile.

"Just promise me, Tess."

"I promise."

"Say it, Tess. 'I'll never go away from you.'"

"I'll never go away from you."

"Promise."

"I promise."

"No matter what."

"No matter what. I promise. I'll never go away from you."

He presses his mouth hard on my temple until it aches. When he pulls away the spot is cold, even colder than the sunny air.

Our good-bye kiss is in front of the MALBA, as the black *remise* draws up to the curb. Lucien walks me to the car. Pushes me back against it. The force is so hard the door handle gouges my lower back. There'll be another flower there.

XLI

I miss him before his plane even leaves the ground. It's Wednesday night, and I lie in bed wishing I were with him. On the far-off wall, the shadows play in a pattern of leaves. The faintest sound of music—it's a ghost of a sound, hardly even audible—floats on the air from the Indians' house and fills me with a longing I almost can't contain.

I wish that I could fly away. I wish I could be with Lucien—tonight and always, wherever he goes. I'm jealous of how he travels and how when he comes back his head is full of memories of places I've never seen. I'm miles from home, from our white house back in Annandale. I'm in another hemisphere, where even the stars have a different look, but now even that is not enough.

I want the life of Lucien. I want to fly away with him and never be left behind again.

XLII

On Thursday it finally happens: Tyler gets his dog. It's the one we saw online the day that we were hanging out. He's been dreaming of her ever since. Flora Dora, though of course, her name is Smoky now. It makes no sense, since she's red and brown with the spikiest fur, but Tyler wants to call her that.

Dad actually took time from work to drive to Tigre to pick her up. He doesn't bother to give another lecture on the Big Responsibility. In the first few hours, Tyler walked Smoky, like, twenty times.

I think he feels old and very proud to be the owner of a dog. Up and down the street they go, stopping off to talk to the *vigilancia* and any neighbors who might be out. None of us have ever met the Indians next door, but through the window I see Tyler talking to one of the gray-haired women. Her saffron sari billows out and her long, fat braid falls forward as she bends to fondle Smoky's head. At first Dad said the dog couldn't sleep in Tyler's bed, but Mom prevailed when she found the two of them entwined—and Tyler smiling in his sleep. Even strict old Dad couldn't hang tough. I should have drawn a picture to show to Lucien next week.

The days go by. For Tyler, everything is great. He runs right home after school each day. He can't wait to see his Smoky Girl. That's what he calls her, Smoky Girl. His friends like to come visit now, especially his new friend Sam. Sam's mom is Anne, the navy wife with seven kids who doesn't have a maid. Maids get in the way, she tells my mom, and they like to do everything by hand—wash your undies, make bread from scratch—why do we have *appliances*? My mom finds that hysterical. Anne, she says, is "such a card."

Anne, my mom, and Sandy Blaine have become, in fact, a little clique. They go shopping together and out to lunch. Sometimes they're there when I get home, gabbing in the living room or, if it's after four o'clock, wrapped up in their sweaters out on the deck, sipping margaritas from the big blue goblets Mom bought just for that. They talk about their kids and school and gossip about the embassy. I know they gossip; I hear the names dropped here and there, their voices dipping between the sips.

Lately they talk about the Ball. It's kind of cute, like they're teenage girls discussing the prom. My mom and Sandy are going to have their dresses made. Anne is going to sew her own. No one can believe it, but Anne sews everything she wears. "You're a nut," Mom tells her, right to her face, and then they all convulse.

They're always laughing, the three of them. They laugh as

much as the perky, happy girls at school—the girls like Cathy and Maureen Fitz—the ones who play sports and don't take art. It makes me feel old to look at them. Like something's wrong with me inside. I feel completely empty. What's the point of anything if Lucien isn't here with me?

It's almost a week and I haven't heard a word from him.

XLIII

The only thing that matters—that has, at least, some little point—is going to the Casa. You wouldn't think a place like that could cheer you up, but somehow it does. I'm not sure why and I can't explain it, but I don't feel empty when I'm there. I almost don't feel anything. I just think of what I'm doing—sewing this button, stringing these beads, gluing pearls on this Styrofoam ball. I guess the mothers feel the same. It's probably why they come. For two short hours, they don't have to feel. They can tune their worries and sadness out.

This week, I actually gave the class. We made tiny marbleized paper books. We did the marbleizing too, rolling the sheets of parchment in baths of water, oil, and paint. It was pleasant to watch the flow of paint and heavy oil, the slow, soft tinting of the page. I wore my beaded dragonfly. I wear it every day—for hope.

XLIV

I know it's only been eight days, but it feels more like a month. I arrive at school with Tyler, and Lucien isn't there. There's an empty space where he ought to be, leaning against the door. I realize I don't have many friends. Yeah, there's Kai and Esme, but my only real friend is Lucien. During the day I try to put circles everywhere—to feel connected, like he said. But I don't feel connected doing that. I only feel more alone. I don't want to admit it to myself, but the truth is there in front of my eyes: Lucien has lied to me. He's broken his promise. He's disappeared.

I start to spend more time at home. Watch all the tricks Tyler's taught to Smoky Girl. My favorite part is watching Tyler demonstrate. "Roll over," he says, and he lies on the ground and shows her how. Sometimes the two of them play so much, the dog's too tired to eat at night.

I catch up on my email, too. Answer Bill's two-line messages and tell him about the dog. I talk to Noree on the phone, and she fills me in on stuff back home. I tell her Lucien's in Rome. But I don't let her know that I haven't heard a word from him. I know what she'd say. And she'd be right.

Mom asks one day if I'll sketch the ball gown that she has in mind. It's that lull in time when the table's set and we're waiting for Dad to get home from work. Tyler's outside with Smoky, and it's very quiet in the house. We go to my room, and I take out my book and pencils. Mom sits on my bed and describes her vision of the dress. It's sort of sweet how excited she is, and it's kind of fun to draw like this. It makes me think of those artists who sketch for the police. *His face was long—no, not that long. And his eyes were squinty. More flat than that.* Only Mom is saying, "The hem fans out, the top goes straight. Yes, straight across." I'm listening hard, trying to see the picture that's inside her head.

Then she says from out of the blue, "So, Tessa, do you still want me to talk to Dad?" For a moment, I'm disconcerted. I'd stopped thinking of that some time ago—of my parents meeting Lucien. So much has happened since that day. I've slept in his bed, I've heard the story of his life, and nothing they could say or do would bring me back to a place where I cared what my father thought. Plus, Lucien is gone. What does it even matter now?

"He's in Europe," I say, scratching away at the hem of the dress. I try to sound really casual. "I don't know when he's coming back."

"What about school?" Mom asks me. The question's so bland and practical, I almost don't know what to say. "School," she repeats. "How can he just take off from school?"

WHEN YOU OPEN YOUR EYES

"His mother thinks that traveling's educational." I scribble some more and don't look up.

"Does he have a father?" she asks me next.

"They're separated. He lives in France."

"That's a shame," she murmurs. Then, after a pause: "Divorce—separation—takes a toll on everyone."

I don't say anything to that. I certainly don't tell her that Lucien's glad his father's gone. Mom would think that's terrible. She still believes that things go on forever. Mom still believes in happiness.

XLV

I guess Dad's work is lightening up. He's been coming home earlier these days. While Mom is fixing dinner (reheating the stuff that Nidia makes), he plays with Tyler or they walk with Smoky down along the riverside.

On Thursday, I go out with them. We stroll along the waterfront. Walk out on the rocks where the waves come in. I look at my dad while we're standing there. I think he's lost a little weight—not that he was heavy—and he looks kind of lean and good. He got a tan in Paraguay. From working "in the field," I guess. It's easier for men, I think. My mom works hard at looking good. There are so many things she does these days—facials, waxings, dyeing her hair. Yet Dad looks younger—who knows why.

The wind is shivering through his hair, which is thick and brown, not a touch of gray, and I find myself wondering certain things that I've never thought about before. Like if women find him handsome. He's sort of all right, I guess you'd say. Kind of strong and straight in that semimilitary way federal agents tend to be. Some women go for that, I guess.

Then another thought comes floating through. I think of him in Bogotá. Two years away from us and Mom. The weekends home were few and short. He must have gotten lonely sometimes. Maybe he really missed us. Maybe he had dreams of us and saw us like that—like a perfect family in a dream that doesn't ever change. Maybe that's why he doesn't get it now.

His gaze is on some far-off boats, their white sails tinted orange as they skim toward shore in the setting sun. He suddenly turns to meet my eyes. He's felt me staring, I can tell. He flashes a smile. "What's up?" he asks. I wonder if I'm crazy, but it almost seems like he feels disarmed. Like he knows what I was thinking—or, knows at least I was thinking of things I'd never thought about him before.

On our way from the park we throw a ball for Smoky. It's monkey-in-the-middle style, and the crazy dog runs back and forth as Tyler pitches to Dad and me. When I miss the ball, Tyler complains that I run like a girl and used to be much faster. It's probably true. I feel like I'm so much older now. And missing Lucien weighs me down.

Back at home, Mom has dinner ready. She's kind of dressed up, it seems to me, in a silky shirt and a bunch of gold and silver beads. There are candles on the table and it's set with the cloth from Paraguay, stiff and white with eyelet holes in the shapes of leaves. I think again about how much effort she's putting in.

How she always seems to be trying so hard to make some picture in her head actually come to life. Everyone is careful. Everyone is so polite. No one wants to spill a drop on the perfect, virgin tablecloth. It's such a pretty picture, but it all feels staged and wrong.

XLVI

It's Saturday night. My parents go out to dinner with Sandy, Anne, and their husbands, Mitch and Tom. Tyler's gone too, spending the night at Sam's house with the neighborhood lady who babysits. It works for me that no one's home. If my parents knew about my plans, they'd lock me in my room.

It's Esme's sixteenth birthday, and Gash is throwing a party for her at a tango club somewhere in San Telmo. He told her to invite some friends, so there's me and Kai and Mitra. (Mitra's precious *novio* agreed to come when he heard that Lucien wouldn't be there. It makes me laugh that Gash is fine, but Lucien's off-limits, ha.) I think Wid's also coming and maybe one other guy. It seems like a night for my big rose dress.

I take a *remise* to Esme's, where all of us are meeting. I phone her from the curbside. I don't want to go into that creepy place. But she tells me to come up; they're having champagne.

At least tonight the apartment doesn't smell so bad. They must have gotten a crew to clean.

Everyone is standing around in the living room, drinking from crystal glasses that look like calla lily stems. Kai and Wid are there. And Esme, of course, the birthday girl. Her hair is tied in pigtails, and she's wearing a short pink dress. She'd look like a child, except for the black around her eyes and the silver snakeskin heels.

"Feliz cumpleaños," I sing at her. I give her the little gift I've brought—a dragonfly brooch I made at home—and in exchange she passes me a small white pill. Wid kisses me too, and Mitra and Kai wag fingers as they come to say hello.

"Hi there, Tessa," says someone else, and, turning, I see Paul. I'm kind of stunned to see him there, but Esme, I guess, has kept in touch. He looks really good, in a crewneck shirt and jacket that show the muscles of his arms. I'm surprised that he remembers my name. I tell him hello. Turn back to Wid. Gash comes slithering into the room. The cats come too, like clouds of dust around his feet. I don't want to look at Gash's feet.

"Daddy," says Esme. "This is Tess."

"Cheerio," Gash calls to me. He's busy uncorking more champagne. Skinny and tall, he crosses the room on stiltlike legs encased in dark blue leather pants. His jacket is black with silver designs—roses, skulls, and rattlesnakes—and his dyed black hair stands up in spikes. I gulp champagne and look away.

"We can leave as soon as Daddy rings," Esme says as she pulls out a phone.

"I thought *I* was your daddy, love." Gash leans forward creepily, tipping his champagne.

"You *are* my daddy, Daddy. I'm talking about my *other* dad. He said he'd ring to wish me happy birthday. He's going to send a present, too."

"Okay, baby," Gash replies. "But we've got to shove off in half an hour."

"No shoving off till Erskine rings."

"Guess I'll sit," Kai comments, flopping on a couch.

"Don't you worry," Esme says. "He's going to call any second now. He said he'd call and I know he will; Erskine doesn't lie to me."

"Not much, he doesn't," murmurs Kai.

"Hey, Tess," says Paul, "how are the marines? Been to any more parties there?"

"That was the one and only time."

"I liked those guys. And I wouldn't mind living in that house—except for the fact that I'd have to enlist."

"Definite drawback."

"Yeah. So where'd you disappear to?"

"What?"

"That night at the party. Where'd you go? That guy came in and suddenly you disappeared." I stand there like a dummy. I don't know what to say to him. I can feel Kai's stare as Paul goes on: "Hope you don't mind my asking. I just liked talking to you, I guess."

I can't believe he's saying this stuff. Paul is old—he's probably almost twenty—and he's magazine-model handsome. His body's so perfect it's almost a joke; the guy plays *polo*, Jesus Christ.

"That's okay," I tell him. Whatever that's supposed to mean. Across the room, Esme's still insisting that Daddy Erskine is going to call, that he never forgets her birthday, and *yes* (to Kai), he knows the date. Paul glances back from her to me.

"He's your boyfriend—that guy who came and took you off?"

I dip to my glass and some fizzy bubbles go up my nose. "Yeah, he is." I almost sneeze.

"Is he coming to this thing tonight?"

"He's out of town. In Italy." I want him to know that Lucien's really somewhere. That he'd be here beside me if he could. Plus it sounds sort of cool to say that he's in Italy.

Then Paul says the craziest thing. And he says it straight and steady like he's stating a simple fact: "If you were my girlfriend, Tessa, I'd take you everywhere I went."

It's awful that Esme's freaking out, but at this moment I'm almost glad she is. Her crazy screams cut the air between Paul and me. Both of us turn to look at her. She's banging her cell phone on the wall. Pieces of it are snapping away, and she's yelping in a high-pitched voice.

"Liar! Liar! You always lie! I hate you! *Hate* you!" *Smash!* goes the entire phone. "You said you'd call! I hope you die!" I feel like I ought to go to her, but it scares me a little how wild she is. I've never seen Esme upset before. Then Gash glides over next to her. He wraps her in his leather arms, whispering stuff against her hair. There's black mascara all over her face, and Gash is wiping it with his sleeve.

"Don't cry, baby," he says to her. "I'm your daddy. I'm the one who loves you. Open your mouth. Yeah, you know how." Her pigtails are a tangled mess, and she's crying like a six-year-old. Gash slips a capsule between her lips. "I'm the one who loves you, babe."

XLVII

We all pile into a *remise* except for Gash and Esme. They take off in his top-down car, an ancient MGB my dad would probably think was cool. I'm squished against Paul and the bulging muscles of his arms. Out the window the city sweeps by—the parklands of Palermo and soon, La Recoleta. *Floralis Genérica*, the huge steel flower sculpture, which opens each day and folds at night, simmers red in its tinted pool, catching soft, reflected glints. We fly along Avenida 9 de Julio in a shining throng of cars past the tall, white obelisk and through the city's heart. Paul directs the driver and we veer to take the scenic routes. The Presidential Palace and the Plaza de Mayo are bathed in a glow of rosy light that seems to linger in the car long after we've passed the sprawling space.

Already Paul's asked if I'm sure I want to do this. We could get our own *remise*, he says, and drive around the city all night. The thought makes my heart beat faster, and for a fleeting moment I picture myself in a car with him as Buenos Aires flickers past the windows. But I tell him no, I want to go to the tango club. It's Esme's birthday, after all.

There's a little pause and then he says, "Her father's a pathetic creep. The bastard couldn't even call?" For a second I'm not sure who he means. Then he adds, "That Gash guy is a sicko too." He stares at me when I don't respond. "Don't tell me you think he's normal and not some kind of perv."

"I don't know," I answer. Because suddenly I don't. "Why are you here if you think he's so bad?"

"I have my reasons. My reason, that is."

I guess he means me, but I don't want to care. Paul isn't really one of us. He may be hot and gorgeous, but there's stuff he doesn't understand. Like how it is with Esme. How she has no family, only us. Maybe Gash really loves her. Maybe it's true that he's the only one who cares.

It's darker in San Telmo, the city's oldest barrio. Catching up with Gash's car, we snake our way through the cobbled streets. Gash parks at the curb, leaving the car in the care of some creep who, for money, promises to keep it safe. He'd rather not park it, he explains, in the area we're headed to. We walk in a clump along the atmospheric streets. There are dim antique shops along the way, their windows full of huge carved chairs and tables, silver and statues, and chandeliers that catch the glint of the flickering *farolas* in their heavy crystal drops. Music drifts from the clubs and bars, and a hum of voices hovers on the plaza in a fog of blurry light.

It's a pretty long walk from the parking spot to the tango

club, and as we go, the neighborhood gets seedier. It's dirty and dark, litter caught in the crevices of the cobblestones. Lots of stuff is going on; you can hear the sounds and music, but it's all inside, just beyond the narrow doors or down the skinny alleys where the light slants out and the echoes play.

From out on the street the tango club reminds me of a cheesy theme park from back at home. The facade sticks out, a wave of bubbly concrete, painted with garish figures of large-breasted women and mustached men. We pass through a velvet curtain into a low-lit space. The section in front is a restaurant, and behind it is the tango club. I can see the slinking shadows, the circular pattern the dancers make as they drag around the floor. The music seeps out, and everything seems to move to it. I feel like I'm sort of slinking too as we walk to the back and squeeze into seats at small round tables against the wall. I'm sitting with Kai and Mitra, one to either side of me. Next to Mitra and her guy are Esme and Gash. Wid and Paul are next to Kai, and Paul keeps craning forward, trying to catch my eye.

The waiter comes by and Gash orders bottles of champagne and a bunch of tapas for everyone. "Today is my birthday," Esme tells the waiter. "And my dad is treating all my friends." I can't read a thing in the waiter's face. But he doesn't ask how old she is. Gash leans over and asks if any of us can dance. His teeth are all weird and crooked, and I think his lips are silicone. "Sillyhead, Daddy!" Esme squeals, acting like herself again.

I turn away from the two of them and look at the dancers on the floor. It's not like the tango you see on *Dancing with the*

Stars; no one's whipping her head around or kicking up her legs. The movements are smooth, hypnotic. The dancers almost seem to crawl, their shadows slender on the wall. They remind me of hounds, stealthy and slow, as they soundlessly circle the lamp-lit room. They move like one single body, slippery, sexy, silent, sad.

XLVIII

I'm high, thank God, by the time Evangeline arrives. I know who she is because Esme squeaks, "Mummy!" and claps her hands. Plus she looks a little bit like Gash. She's stalky and thin with black spiked hair and is wearing a backless dress. She's a hundred years old, so you can imagine how good that looks. Underneath she's wearing a bra—a regular bra—stretched across the backless part. The bra is red and doesn't look new. She must be totally out of her mind. Gash pulls out their table and she sits on Esme's other side. There's a shifting of chairs, and Paul is suddenly next to me.

"Everyone!" calls Esme. "This is my mum—Evangeline." I hear Paul make a quiet groan. The woman smiles, smeary lipstick on her teeth. She nibbles on a piece of roasted pepper and starts looking around the room at men. It's more than looking, really—she's doing something with her mouth, something I don't want to see.

One of the men comes over. He's three hundred pounds, dressed all in white like he thinks that we're in Panama. He

WHEN YOU OPEN YOUR EYES

stands there gazing down at her, and she climbs to her feet and follows him to the floor. The music's about to start again. They stare into each other's faces. Nobody blinks; it's like a duel. An opening chord and they glare a second longer. Then his paw clamps tightly on her waist, and the two of them slide away.

"Look at Mum," says Esme. She sidles her chair back up to Gash. Together they watch as Mummy circles round and round. Esme starts to kiss his neck.

"Want to dance?" Paul asks me.

"I don't know how."

"Just fake it."

"How do you fake the tango?" To me it looks like a serious dance. Like you couldn't just do it on the spot.

"Just let me lead. That's really what it's all about."

"I'd look like an idiot," I say.

"You wouldn't—you couldn't," Paul replies. I feel my blush like a wave of heat. I really wish I did know how to tango. It would be nice to move around and have a change of scenery. Esme's still kissing Gash's neck. Her soft pink mouth on the reptile skin. Out on the floor Evangeline keeps dancing with Mr. Panama. Her dress slits high on her long, thin legs. The skin near her knees hangs loose like cloth. If Lucien were here with me, it would all be a joke, like kitschy art. He'd totally love Evangeline. Her dyed black hair. Her made-up face. He'd absolutely love her bra. He'd want to do a sketch of Gash.

All of a sudden some woman comes over and glares at Paul. That's how they ask in tangoland. She's thirty years old, if anything, and Paul is getting to his feet. He shoots me a glance as if to say *If you won't dance, there are others who will.* I watch him go, leading her to the floor. He knows how to do it—all of it. The pause, the stare, the taking of her narrow waist. I don't want to look, but I can't stop. The woman is tall, with beautiful legs, and is wearing red high heels. As she swirls around, Paul looks beyond her head at me. Right at my face with eyes he must think smoldering. Kai sees too and chuckles.

"While the cat's away . . ."

"It's not like that. I didn't know Paul would be here. Esme never told me. Esme never—"

Kai tosses back her dark red hair. "Take it easy, will you, Tess?"

I've suddenly started thinking of the sunlit day I said good-bye to Lucien. Standing outside the MALBA when he made me promise all those things. No dangerous jaunts with Esme. No seedy bars with Kai or Wid. And out of nowhere: *Don't see Paul.* And here I am—doing every last thing I promised that I wouldn't do. The truth of this hits me, and I actually have to touch my mouth to keep the little gasp held in. I suddenly feel extremely sick.

"I'll be right back," I say to Kai, though I know I'm cutting out of there.

"I didn't mean anything by—"

"It's okay. I'll be right back." I grab my purse and shove away before she has time to stop me. I know that she is watching, so I pause and ask a waiter for directions to the ladies' room.

I follow his pointed finger, then backtrack out the door. I run to the corner under a light and dial for a *remise*.

Music floats from balcony windows overhead. There's a hum of voices from somewhere not too far away—there must be a plaza or a giant, open restaurant. Some couples drift by, and the women give me a lingering look, as if to ask what I'm doing here.

Glancing back toward the tango club, I suddenly see Paul. He's standing out front, searching in all directions, and I know it's me he's looking for. I think I hear him call my name, and I take a step back to hide in the recess of a door.

XLIX

M y mom comes in my bedroom wrapped in her long pink robe.

"It's late," she says.

"I know it is."

"Have you been drinking, Tess?" she asks. I decide not to lie. Sort of.

"We had champagne to celebrate Esme's birthday. I only had a glass or two. I guess I'm just a wimp."

"I suppose it's all right. For a birthday toast."

"What about you? Did you have a good time?"

"Yes, we did. It was really nice." She's looks so cozy in her robe. So clean and soft and comfortable. It's the craziest thing: I'm jealous. I wish that I could be my mom. Sleepy and soft, going back to a bed in a sweet pink robe. It's lucky I even made it home. The driver couldn't find me, and I waited more than half an hour. Kai had come out to talk to Paul. Then she went back in, and Paul took off down a different street.

Once in the car I kind of zoned out. I was high on champagne and hadn't eaten very much. I only knew I was close to home by the rhythm of the flicking light. I know it by heart, the spacing of the traffic lights, the buzzing neon in the stores. When I looked out the murky window we were passing the Naval Academy. The shadows of the palm trees swayed on the moonstruck white facade, and a band of *cartoneros* was gathering scrap in front of the gate. They looked like ghouls, dragging cardboard boxes and their rickety carts piled high with junk.

I checked my email when I got home. My outbox was full of emails from me, but there wasn't a word from Lucien. Maybe I deserve it after all the things I did tonight.

L

I have a headache Sunday. It whines, not pounds, which maybe champagne headaches do. Church, again, is a kind of relief. I sit in the pew in the streaming light and pray to God to forgive me for lying to Lucien. I didn't mean to (I say to God) and I swear on the hymnal on my lap that I'll never lie to him again. And while I'm at it: *Please, please let him love me still.*

At breakfast, my parents chat with their new best friends, the Blaines and the McDermotts. The McDermotts have joined our fabulous church. Their seven kids are with them, all spruced up, wearing little bow ties and sweaters their mother made by hand. The girls wear ironed dresses. They have long, neat braids with those little ball ties on the tips. It makes me tired to think of all that knitting, that tying of ties and braiding of hair. I can't even run my one small life. I start to pray all over again.

Tomorrow is Monday. Oh my God. Tomorrow Lucien comes home.

LI

Except that it doesn't happen. Lucien doesn't show at school. I get all dressed up in my *Standing Girl in Green* shirt. I put on special makeup. Something smudgy around my eyes. I'm the girl in the painting. He loves that girl. I'm walking so fast, Tyler can't keep up with me. "Slow down," he begs, but I won't slow down; I can't slow down. We get to the school and I see him there—my *mind*, I mean, actually sees him standing there. *Grand-père*'s sweater. Tumbling curls. I'm stunned when the picture fades away and all that's left is air. I wait and wait. A kind of panic starts to whirl. He isn't coming; I know he's not.

Tuesday, Wednesday. He doesn't come back. People ask me where he is. Esme. Kai. Mrs. Pasacalia. At first I was only scared for me, but now I'm terrified for him. Even the school hasn't heard a word. Something's happened. Something bad. I send him another message. I've already sent twelve, but I don't care. I don't hear anything back from him. There's no one to ask and I'm losing my mind.

❦❦❦

A whole week passes, and the following Monday I get an email from Solange. It was sent from her embassy address. I almost can't breathe as I open it.

Dear Tessa,

I know you are very worried about Lucien. He is well. He is with his father in Paris, where he will be staying for some time. I am sorry, at the moment I cannot tell you more.

Solange L. du Previn

LII

It's three weeks now since he's been gone. The buds of the jacarandas are fat and purple and ready to burst, and flowers are blooming in the yard—hibiscus and bright pink cyclamen, impatiens in their frilly clumps. My dad has filled the swimming pool. It looks like a giant turquoise jewel shimmering in the sun. The Indians next door to us sit for hours in their plastic chairs. I see them through the chinks of hedge in their pastel-colored saris—rose and yellow and apple-green. Sometimes they wash their hair outdoors and dry it, shining, in the sun. Sam McDermott is here a lot. He and Tyler tear around, Smoky leaping at their heels. The late-spring light falls into my room and plays like water on the floor. It's almost *trompe l'oeil*. My room's the pond. My bed a big fat lily pad where I float and dream of Lucien.

I wrote to Solange, but she never wrote back. I think it's very cruel of her.

Dear Mrs. du Previn,

Thank you for your email. You're right that I was worried. I'm so glad to hear that Lucien is fine. I don't understand what's happened, though, and I really need to hear from him. Could you please allow him to email me or send me his address in France? I can hardly sleep and I think about him all day long.

So please just let me contact him. I'd be very grateful to you for that.

Sincerely,
Tessa Logan

LIII

It's possible Kai feels sorry for me. She suggests we go out on Friday night. This is very un-Kai, and I'm sort of touched. She tells me to meet her at her place, and I take a *remise* into Palermo, where she lives. When I get there, her parents are having a party on the roof of their apartment. All the guests are speaking Dutch, and everyone looks related, like members of one giant tow-haired family. Kai's big blond dad is sweating over the sizzling *parilla*, joking with friends as he flips the steaks and lamb chops and rolls chorizo over the flames.

Kai brings me over to meet her mom. She looks just like her husband, big-boned and blond with ruddy skin, and she's leaning back against the terrace railing, drinking beer from a bottle and talking with friends. She knows my mom from the women's club, but somehow we've never met.

"Ah, Tessa. Hello! So glad you could come. Edda, Beatrice— this is Tess, Kai's American friend from school."

The other guests are friendly, and Beatrice asks in a hearty voice, "So how do you like life in Buenos Aires?"

"It's great," I say.

"Yeah," she agrees. "Wid loves it too. We were in Malawi before we came here. For us it's simply paradise." It's only then that I notice Wid standing across the patio. So Beatrice is his mother. It's funny; you can't really picture him having one. He's dressed in his usual scruffy style—shabby T-shirt and jeans cut off below the knees. His hair pokes out like the bristles of a scrub brush, pale and dusty brown. He's chugging beer with a guy about his mother's age. I go over to say hello to him, and he's deep in conversation about Argentina's Dirty War.

"You'd be dropped from a plane," says the older man, pulling a pack of cigarettes from the pocket of his shirt. "Students. Professors. Artists. Anyone with 'subversive thought.'"

"Tess lives near the naval school where they used to torture prisoners," Wid tells the guy, without even saying hi to me. I think it's cool that Wid and this guy, who's really old, are chatting away like equals—that the guy's not talking down to him as my parents' friends tend to do with me—but I don't want to hear what they have to say. I've read about the Dirty War, the decade in the seventies and eighties when a *junta* ruled the country and thousands of people were kidnapped, tortured, and "disappeared." But Buenos Aires is just so beautiful to me, and part of me can't believe that stuff. Either way, I don't want to think of it tonight. I turn away from Wid and the man, and gaze beyond the rooftop's edge.

"Want to get out of here?" murmurs Kai, coming up beside me. It's weird how I sort of don't want to leave. I like the view and the mellowness of the atmosphere. No one would care if Kai and I started drinking beer. Over the scent of roasting meat, a hint of marijuana floats, slender as a thread. But for Kai, I guess, this is as bad as Chatter Night. "By the way—" She digs into the pocket of her jeans and pulls a slip of paper out. "Paul asked if I would give you this."

"What is it?"

"What else—his number. Take it, Tess. You never know." She presses the paper into my hand. "He likes you a lot. He went after you the other night when you ran out of the tango club."

"You know that I'm with Lucien."

"Really? Where is he?"

"He's coming back."

"He might." Kai shrugs. "Or again, he might not. Either way, believe me, you'd be better off with Paul—"

"But Lucien's the one I love!"

Kai laughs at that, but not a funny-ha-ha laugh. "Are you sure you really know him, Tess?"

"What is that supposed to mean?"

"Just keep Paul's number," Kai replies. "Stick it in your bag." I could ask her more, but it's clear that's all she wants to say. Plus it's probably all I want to hear. Kai doesn't get it. She never will. I shove the paper into my purse in the slot with the little pills.

Down on the street, Kai shakes herself as if to brush something off her skin. "It was hot up there," she mumbles. "My parents' friends all talk too much. And I hate the smell of meat." I turn around to answer her and a sudden thought flies into my mind: Her hair is dyed that deep wine-red. How could I not have known that? She's blonde like her parents underneath and doesn't want to look like them.

We go to a club and she flirts in Spanish to get us in. The music pounds—Brazilian techno, way too loud—and the place is dark with crazy, multicolored strobes that zap like hot electric shocks. It isn't possible to talk, and I think that's why she's picked this place. Everyone talks too much for Kai. And she doesn't want me to talk, for sure. She'd have to listen if I did.

LIV

Mom comes home with Sandy and Anne. She's just picked up her gown, and her friends can hardly contain themselves. She hollers up the stairs to me.

"Tessa, come see! I've got the dress!" When I come down, she's standing in the living room holding a long white garment bag. Anne has called the boys inside—as if Tyler and Sam want to see a dress. Even Smoky has come along to watch. Nidia takes the garment bag and slowly Mom unzips. Ripples of blue come pouring out.

"Isn't it gorgeous?" Sandy cries.

Mom turns to me, her face all flushed. "Tessa, honey, what do you think?"

"It looks like a waterfall," I say. "Really, Mom, it's beautiful."

The pleasure deepens on her face, and Nidia echoes, "Beautiful," carefully forming the English word. She's touching the gown in an almost reverential way. Like Cinderella stroking the hem of a dress she'll never get to wear.

"Try it on," Anne urges. "Everyone wants to see." Mom grabs

the bag and starts for the stairs. "Nidia, darling, *por favor*—" She calls in Spanish for snacks and margaritas, and tells me to bring her friends outside. I lead them out to the tables and chairs on the patio, near the swimming pool. It's warm and bright, a beautiful, waning afternoon. The refreshments come out before my mom. I make small talk with Anne and Sandy. Stuff about school and Christmas break. Anne remarks that I've lost some weight. I'm starting to get squirmy when finally my mom comes out.

She's standing just outside the door, and the sun is slanting across her hair and the plane of her chest where the fabric cuts a clear straight line. Her skin is tawny in the light and she's pinned up her hair so her neck looks long and graceful. When she walks across the patio, the cloth of the dress ripples just like water, the deeper blue running to aqua at the edge. She looks so pretty it takes my breath.

That night she hangs the dress in my room.

"It's silly," she says as we hook the bag on my closet door, "but I don't want Jim to see it. I want to surprise him the night of the ball." She calls him "Jim" instead of "Dad," almost like I'm her friend. It's funny, though; I'm not her friend. Not anymore. If we were friends I'd have talked to her about Lucien. I'd have told her that I loved him. That he was my boyfriend now, not Mike. She'd have known that he had not come back from Italy, and that I was scared to death. I don't even think she remembers that he went away. So caught up in her fairy-tale ball, she has no idea what's going on. No idea there's a giant hole in the center of my life.

LV

Even my real friend, Noree, doesn't know what's going on. I just don't want to write the words. I know what she'll say about Lucien: that something's off and I'd better watch out. She knows about the last time he went MIA. Open your eyes and *look*, she'd say. I can almost hear the sensible words coming out of her mouth. I don't want to hear what I already know, so I just don't tell her anything. Sometimes I go to her Facebook page and on her wall write stupid stuff that makes it sound like everything's fine. *It's summer here, ha, ha,* I wrote, and *Polo players are not so hot.*

Today she's posted a bunch of pictures from the Halloween Ball at school. It's not a ball like the one my mom is going to; it's a costume party they have each year at Annandale High. I look at the shots. The first shows our school in a blaze of red and yellow trees. It all looks so familiar—the low brick building, the grassy field, the pathways spattered with fallen leaves— that I feel a pang of memory. The next one shows the doors of the gym; they're held open with bales of hay and the beat-up scarecrows they use each year. There's a scene of the gym's interior, the walls all draped with spiderwebs and ghosts made of plastic garbage bags. The decorations never change. I bet that twenty years from now, the same old stuff will be hanging from the rafters there.

Next are pictures of kids dressed up in costumes. A viking. A ghoul. A white-faced bride all covered in blood. There's someone in a burka and next to her is an Arab sheik. The sheik is tall and wearing glasses above his beard. There's something familiar about this sheik.

I look more closely at the girl. She's covered up from head to toe with just a slit in the veil for eyes. Yet I know it's Norah. Even faceless, I can tell. That's how well I know my Nor. The guy in the robe, the sheik—is Mike.

It doesn't take long to figure out what's going on. Some kids have posted on the wall.

Forbidden love. Isn't it cute?
What can you do underneath a burka?

LVI

I'm lying in bed trying to picture Lucien. His mouth and eyes and the sexy tumble of his curls. But it isn't Lucien I see. Instead it's Mike drifting across my eyelids, floating on the soft black screen. I'm thinking of stuff he used to do—how he'd double-check my seat belt, close the button of my coat at the puniest little breeze. He was always so protective, and I always felt very safe with him. No harm could come with Mike around.

It's really different with Lucien. It's more like *I* take care of *him*. At first I didn't realize this. He seemed so free and self-assured. The whole world seemed to belong to him. But now I know it isn't like that. He said it himself. He needs me to help him "stay intact."

And then I think of Noree. Her face comes gliding onto the screen—that impish face with the three dark freckles on her cheek and the swing of chestnut hair. I'm so confused by what I feel. I don't want Mike. I'm the one who ended it, but it doesn't mean I want him to be with someone else. Especially Noree, my bestest friend from the age of six. I tell myself that if Lucien were here with me, I wouldn't really care. But he isn't here, and I'm all alone, and Noree and Mike are a unit now and I'm not a part of what they are together and nothing will ever be the same.

LVII

I 've got to show you something, Tess!" Kai grabs my arm as I walk into school. Her cheeks are pink and she's bursting with excitement, which isn't like her at all. Esme's in tow, looking half-asleep.

"It's a mystery," she murmurs, shrugging. Her uniform blouse is inside out. "She won't explain it. We have to *see*."

"That's right," says Kai. "You need the graphics for this one, guys." We follow her down the hallway and into the computer lab. She seats herself at one of the desks and quickly goes online. "I only found it by accident. I wasn't looking for anything. Just bored last night and playing around. Then all of a sudden—" She jabs at the computer keys. "Take a look at this."

I stare at the screen as a blog pops up. "It's Italian," she says. "But I'll translate for the two of you." An image appears. Something I have seen before. A famous fountain in Italy. The one on all the postcards with Neptune and his horses and the little sea gods everywhere. *Fontana di Trevi*—the name hangs over the murky blog. And underneath: *Trevi en Bleu.*

"So what?" I say. "What does it mean?"

"Listen," snaps Kai. "And *look*." She leans in close and starts to read, translating as she goes. "Rome, November twenty-one. In the predawn hours, a self-described 'guerilla' dumped packets of brilliant cyan dye into the Trevi Fountain. Within moments, according to a witness, the dye began to . . . I don't know . . . disperse . . . I guess. By sunrise the waters of Rome's most famous fountain were a bright and . . . something . . . Caribbean blue.

"Leaflets left behind by the *'artist'*—(quotation marks around the word)—explain the act as a 'protest against gray bourgeois society.' Four years ago, another vandal left similar notes after dousing the fountain with blood-red dye." Here Kai pauses to take a breath.

"The underage culprit has not been identified in the press, but reliable sources indicate that he is the son of a VIP in the cultural ministry of France and a prominent Paris barrister. The boy was arrested and charged with vandalism. He was not detained and has left the country in the custody of his parents. What will come next—a *Trevi en Violet*?"

I stare at the picture on the screen. "Lucien doesn't talk like that. 'Gray bourgeois society.' I'm sure it isn't—"

"It's him, all right," Kai snaps at me.

"But why would he do a thing like that?"

"He's going off again, I guess."

"What do you mean he's 'going off'?" Kai looks at me with a mix of amusement and disbelief.

"Sometimes, Tess, I wonder where you come from. I mean,

how you can be so damn naive? Don't you know anybody daft?"

"I may be naive," I rasp at her, "but Lucien isn't daft!" I've never said "daft" in all my life, and the word sounds weird coming out of my mouth; it hovers, blimplike, in the air.

"He's a little bipolar," Esme says. "But I think the fountain looks pretty blue." I turn from Kai to Esme. I can't believe she knows the word "bipolar." Another blimp, it hangs in the air with "daft."

Kai speaks in a slightly gentler voice. "Actually, he's been very normal the past few months. I think that you've been good for him."

"Me?"

"Yes, you. You keep him on an even keel. He never should have gone to Rome."

There are so many questions I want to ask, but Kai's already called me naive. Plus I don't want to hear her harsh, predictable take on things. I don't believe he's crazy. I think that something happened in Rome. I remember what he told me about breaking things when his *grand-père* died. It wasn't crazy to do those things; I think it showed how sane he was. Why is it normal to sit and do nothing when someone dies and your whole world suddenly falls apart?

"That's why he didn't come back," says Kai.

"Do you think he's in jail?" breathes Esme. "Lucien wouldn't be fond of jail."

"Didn't you listen to what I read? 'He was not detained and has left the country in the custody of his parents.' He's in France with his father. That's where he is!" Kai acts as if she's cracked the case of the century. (I never told her I'd heard from Solange and actually knew where Lucien was.) She looks at the screen and shakes her head. "His mother could lose her job for this. His father might put him in boarding school."

"What's the problem?" Esme sighs. "I really like the fountain blue."

"It's centuries old," Kai snaps at her. "It's marble. It's art. Lucien's an idiot." She flicks her hair and turns to me. "Don't say I didn't warn you, Tess."

LVIII

There's an email from Norah in my box. It's been there for at least a week.

Hi Tess,

Have you been to my Facebook lately? If you have, I'm sure you saw the messages. I really wanted to tell you first, but the gossip got ahead of me. Anyway, it's true. Mike and I started going out. At first we were scared that it might not be ok with you. And I promise you, Tess, if I thought you cared for him at all, I'd never have even looked at him. But you're so in love with L that I figured it would be all right. It is, Tess, isn't it? Tell me yes. He's really sweet and I like him a lot. To tell u the truth, I liked him when u were with him, but I never let u know.

Please write back as soon as u can.

Love,
Noreee

I don't write back. I don't know what to say to her.

LIX

In the middle of the drama, we celebrate Thanksgiving. Mom and her friends get the big idea to do the traditional turkey thing, and Anne McDermott offers her house. Of all the people to volunteer—the one and only person in the suburbs of Buenos Aires who doesn't have a maid. I'll probably end up having to wash the dishes. The McDermotts live in a *barrio encerrado*. That means "gated community." Guards with machine guns greet us at the ivy-covered entrance booth. Dad shows ID, but they phone the McDermotts just to make sure.

To get to the house, we wind our way through a maze of shady, tree-lined streets. "How pretty," says Mom, gazing out the window at the sprawling homes and yards. Dad remarks that the wave of crime after the economic fall made people want to protect themselves, and places like this got popular. I think it has to do with toys. There are toys and bikes all over the lawns, and I think the people came here so their kids could leave their stuff outside and not have it stolen during the night.

"We're here," says Mom, motioning toward a big brick

house. There are lots of cars parked around the cul-de-sac. A silky flag emblazoned with a turkey hangs over the McDermotts' door, flapping faintly in the breeze. The other guests are already there. The Blaines, of course, and the Muldoons and the Fitzes and Mrs. McKnight. The kids are all scattered in various groups, and Tyler quickly runs off with Sam, Smoky close behind. It was nice of them to invite the dog.

I wander around from room to room, not sure where I ought to go. I'm thinking, of course, of Lucien. I never stop thinking of Lucien. He'd laugh if he ever saw this place. There are fake Impressionist paintings hanging on almost all the walls—a famous Monet of women in a garden and some Degas ballerinas in fancy golden frames.

Beyond the window, the scene is anything but French. All the men are out in the yard playing football on the lawn. Cathy's brother Jason is holding the ball above his head getting ready to make a pass. Maureen's brothers are also there, and Greg Muldoon, who's in my class. Tyler and Sam are dancing around like monkeys, and the older guys, including Dad, are all prepared to leap. It strikes me again how young Dad looks, especially next to the other dads who have a little paunch in front and get red in the face if they run too much. I don't know why it bothers me that he seems to look younger every time I turn around.

For a while I hang around upstairs in the giant, dormlike playroom with the little McDermott girls. It's fun at first, as they show me all their toys and stuff. They're crazy for dolls and each has a prized American Girl. The dolls' clothes, of course, are all homemade, and so are the accessories. Their beds, for example, are really cardboard boxes, and the tables are books set on top of empty cans. But every bed has a crocheted quilt, and flowers from the garden sit in jars on the improvised dish-towel table-cloth. It's kind of cool, the things they have invented, and it makes me remember playing dolls with Norah. Once we made her Barbie die and buried her in a coffin we'd built from an old Saran Wrap box.

Yet after some time in the cluttered room, I start to get claustrophobic. The dolls, which look just like their owners—that's the idea of American Girls—suddenly seem like tiny clones, and the room feels so crowded I have to get out.

In the kitchen, of course, all the moms are hanging around—Sandy, Anne, my mom, Greg's mom, Liz, and Maureen's mom, Diane. Mrs. McKnight sits in a nearby chair. Cathy and Maureen are there, pretending to be useful, wiping off some serving spoons. Everybody's brought a dish and most of the food is already in the oven, so no one's really working now. They're just hanging out, sipping Blood Marys in the huge, hot room that smells like butter and cloves and pie.

It's just like Thanksgiving back at home. All the relatives from both sides of the family would come to dinner at our house. The women and girls would hang out in the kitchen while the guys watched football on TV or played outside, just like they are doing now. I really used to like that. And maybe I'd enjoy this, too, if I weren't missing Lucien. Everyone seems to have a place, but I don't feel like part of any group. Everyone's with the people they love most on earth, but Lucien's far away from me somewhere in France with his angry dad.

"Tessa, hi!" my mom calls out before I can turn around and flee. Her voice sounds loud and hyper—like she hasn't seen me for several weeks. Everyone turns to say hello and ask me where I've been. I tell them I was with the girls, playing with their dolls. Her parents bought those dolls, says Anne; she'd never buy "gimmicky" dolls like them—though the girls adore them, she has to admit.

Then: "Oh!" she cries. "I have a job for the three of you." She means Cathy, Maureen, and me. She passes Cathy a pile of paper turkeys and gives Maureen a pen. The turkeys are really place cards; she wants us to do the seating plan.

The tables are set in the dining room, a separate one for the little kids with a paper pilgrim centerpiece. I let Cathy and Maureen take charge, and walk around the table putting the turkeys wherever they say.

"Where do you want to sit?" Maureen asks as she scrawls my name.

"I don't care," I tell her.

"Yeah," she says. "I guess it's a little dull for you. I mean, no one you really know is here."

"It isn't dull. I think it's nice."

"But *they'd* be bored," says Cathy. "I'm sure they don't do stuff like this—Esme and Kai and—"

Maureen blurts out, "Where is Lucien these days? Is it true he isn't coming back?"

"Where did you hear that?" I ask. I set down a place card and try to make my voice sound calm.

"I don't know. Just around."

"We thought you'd know," says Cathy. "Aren't you sort of—"

"We're friends," I say. I don't want them telling their mothers stuff. Though I'm sure they know I'm lying. They see the way we are at school.

"I sure couldn't picture Lucien here," Maureen puts in with a glance around the dining room.

"Or out in the yard," says Cathy, "playing football with the guys." She places my card a mile away from where she and Maureen are sitting by the mountainous bowl of gourds. I don't go back to the kitchen with them.

I'm starting to feel like the walls are closing in on me, and I want to get back to my own true life. The life I have with Lucien. I feel like I'm going to scream or cry, and I wonder how I'm going to last through dinner. And then I remember something. The thought of it gives me instant hope, and I hurry off to find my bag.

There are still a few pills in the zippered slot. By now I know which ones are best, and I pluck a little blue one out. It's an OxyContin, the tiniest dose. I swallow it in the bathroom. Then I wander back outside again. I sit in a chair in the grassy yard and wait to feel the numbness, the blurring of the pain.

LX

J ason has the ball again. He passes it for Dad to catch, and a
shaft of sun falls into my eyes as I tip my head to watch. Dad
leaps into the yellow light. For a second he seems suspended.

His body's so lean and graceful, he looks like the angel
Michael flying through the air. But then I see his face. His throat
is clenched; the muscles bulge like tightened ropes. His forehead is creased with lines of strain, and I realize how much it
means to him—how fast he runs, how good he looks, how surely
he catches the twirling ball in hands that seem outstretched in
prayer. He catches the ball and lands on earth, and Maureen's
dad jogs after him. But no one can catch my driven dad, my
desperate-looking, driven dad, tearing across the trampled grass.
Jason runs to meet him in and they punch each other and do
high fives as if they've just won the world.

At dinner I'm fine. I'm warm and numb. I sit through grace,
which goes on and on as everyone adds the items they're most
grateful for. When my turn comes, I say I'm grateful for "being

here" and everyone thinks that I mean *here*, at Mrs. McDermott's table with the turkey, which wasn't a simple thing to find (there was only one left at Carrefour), and all these nice Americans, including my lovely family, my brother and Mom and my handsome dad, who looks younger and newer every day (though now I know he works at it, maybe even harder than my mom). My dad, in fact, makes his prayer about Mom. Well, first he says he's grateful for his family, passing a glance at each of us. Then he says that there wouldn't be a family if it weren't for his "amazing wife." For two whole years, he tells the group, she kept the family going completely on her own. "At this point," he says, "I'm sort of an accoutrement—like that antique lamp you keep around but hardly ever use."

Everyone laughs, and Mom, of course, who's blushing, says, "Jim, you know that isn't true."

I look at Dad. They've placed him next to Liz Muldoon, who's a single mom and younger than the rest of them. She throws back her hair and smiles at him, and I can't believe my football-catching father feels anything like a lamp.

At dinner I chat with Mrs. McKnight, whom Cathy decided to sit me with. No one knows how high I am because they're all high on wine themselves. There's pie for dessert, apple and pumpkin with *dulce de leche* on the side. There's ice cream and whipped cream in big white bowls. Chocolate turkeys wrapped in foil. I help clear off the table. I load the dishwasher with my mom. She's wearing an apron over her dress, gingham with an apple print. And everything feels just fine. I'm grateful, so grateful. *Gracias*, Gash.

❧❧

In the middle of the night I wake. Consciousness slips over me and with it comes the sinking crash. It's like I'm falling into a hole, a bottomless and lightless hole. The drop makes me dizzy and slightly sick. *"Lucien,"* I whisper, and I swoop even deeper into the dark.

LXI

I'm going to telephone Solange. I'm going to make her see me—in person, I mean—so she has to tell me what's going on. And just when I've decided this, when I trash the email I'd started to write and move to make the phone call, Lucien's message comes flying in.

Tess, ma belle, I'm back. I need to see u. When can we meet?

I don't even think as I text him back.

Now.

The statue of Juan Pablo.

What?

Biblioteca Nacional. Half an hour. Go around back.

He's gone before I answer. I don't have a clue where he's talking about, but I'm so excited I don't care. I'll just tell the driver when he comes. Biblioteca Nacional. I wear my jeans and the shirt he likes. At least, he used to like this shirt. My parents are out with Tyler, which is very good since I'm too upset and nervous to tell a decent lie. In the car I think about what I'll say. And then I decide I won't say anything at all. I'll wait till he tells me everything. I won't interrupt. I'll wait until I hear it all. I will not say *I can't believe you lied to me.*

The drive from the suburbs takes forever this afternoon. The length of highway that runs along the slums of Villa 31 seems to stretch for endless miles. Above the sprawl of makeshift shacks, the skyline of the city looms, bright and silver in the sun. My eyes get caught in the tangled streets of the *villa miseria.* The complicated labyrinths, garbage strewn and full of hidden dangers, seem to mirror my life with Lucien.

At last, in La Recoleta the driver stops at the door of the National Library. It's a modern-looking building, which I've never visited before. When I walk around to the side of it, I see the statue of the pope. It's massive and tall, and his miter looks gold where it stabs the sky. I'm sweating like mad, and my legs feel sluggish when I move. I feel as if I'm wearing Juan Pablo's heavy robe.

For a minute I stop to gather my breath. I'm afraid of myself—that I'll cry or scream when I see his face. Part of me wants to do that. To scream at him for breaking his word and disappearing from me again. And then I see him and everything stops.

My rage goes dead, and I feel the halting of my heart. I'm frozen in place as I watch him appear from the shadow of the monument and lift his face to search for mine. He freezes too; I see it in his body. And for several stock-still seconds we stand at a distance, looking straight into each other's eyes.

Neither is the first to move. We move together. In synchrony. It's almost as if we have one mind. It triggers and we start to run, and crash into each other's arms at the feet of the sunstruck pope.

LXII

We sit on the grassy slope underneath a tree. All around, people are basking in the sun. Dog walkers, a common sight wherever you go, are chatting together with their packs. The dogs seem to talk among themselves, their leashes wound around the trees. As we sit in the cheery atmosphere, I learn that Lucien was depressed. Really depressed, so he had to see a doctor and take some kind of drugs. He's thinner. I felt his slightness in my arms. "It happens sometimes," he tells me. "I didn't want for you to know."

"Well, I wish I had," I say to him. "It would have helped me understand." I hope that's true. I hope I would have understood, because even now I still don't see why he couldn't have sent a word to me. "I thought you'd be happy in Rome," I say. "I thought you really wanted to go."

"I did," he says. "I didn't know my father was going to meet us there."

"Your father showed up in Rome?"

Lucien nods. "He came to have a talk with me. He thought the timing would be good, and he liked the 'neutral setting.' The talk was all about my life. My current schooling and plans for university. None of these plans were made by me. My father's decided I have to follow the family path—and he wants me back in France."

"What do you mean, 'the family path'?"

"International studies. Like *Maman*."

"But you're an artist, Lucien—"

"Art is a hobby, my father says. *Grand-père* made paintings on the side, but he also had a 'real' career."

"And your mother lets him talk like that, when she's the cultural attaché?"

"She can't stop my father's talk. 'I won't have any son of mine going through life like a vagabond.'"

"But Lucien, it's not his life! He can't tell you what to do with it."

Lucien smiles. "I said the same. Then everything, of course, blew up. I'd have no life, he told me, if *he* didn't work the way *he* does. *Maman* was furious at this, and let him know *Grand-père* had left me money and we didn't need his anymore."

"Wow, that's great—and good for her."

"It wasn't good for her at all. The fight got very terrible—and, as always, because of me. I left the hotel. I was so enraged and I had to respond in a violent way. I wanted to do some violent *art* so my father would see the power, how big and important art can be." He stops for a moment to take a breath. "So then I have this big idea that will get in all the newspapers, be seen on YouTube and everywhere else. Someone did it once before, but I will do it differently. Wait till I you hear what I—"

"I know what you did," I say to him. My voice is flat compared to his. "Kai saw the picture on a blog."

"A picture of—?"

"Yes. The fountain."

"Really? Oh well, I am not surprised. There were people taking pictures. They interviewed me on TV." There's pleasure in his narrowed eyes. "So everybody knows?"

"I don't know who else Kai showed it to. Because of your age, your name wasn't mentioned on the blog."

"It was my father who quashed my name." Lucien's voice takes a bitter edge. "He paid through the nose. That's all he kept saying for two whole weeks: 'I paid through the nose, I'll have you know.' He paid to have everything hushed up."

"But, Lucien, what about your mother? Wouldn't it—" I stop before I say what Kai suggested—that it might have jeopardized her job. I also don't say that he's jeopardized us; that if my dad ever heard what he'd done, well, forget about any meeting, any friendly dinner my mom might plan.

"Yes, she was upset," he says. "That's why she sent me back to France. That was a way to punish me. But then I got sick, and it didn't matter anymore."

"What didn't matter?"

"Whatever I did. At the end of two weeks, I called her from my father's house and told her she had to come for me. I told her I was so depressed that if she didn't come for—"

I feel like I know what he's going to say, and I don't want to hear the words. "Lucien, stop."

"I'm sorry, Tess." He suddenly takes my hand in his. It's the first time we've touched since our embrace, and his fingers feel thin and cold. "It isn't easy to be with me. And I'd understand if you wanted to go."

"I don't want to go. But I—"

"Thank God," he says, and his head falls, heavily, into my chest. I bury my chin in his windblown curls and hold him very close. I want to soothe and help him. But the truth of it is, I don't know how.

A little bipolar, Esme had said, she and Kai staring into my face, amused at how naive I am. They were right; I am naive. I know about people being depressed. I have been depressed myself. But I never knew anyone sick with it. I mean, clinically sick, so sick and sad that the person you love, who loves you more than she loves herself, can't make you want to live. I can't imagine feeling like that. No matter how sad and bleak I got, I'd never hide from Lucien.

But then I remember that Lucien's "daft." I can hear Kai's voice inside my head. That's what the fountain was all about— that's the hyper, manic side, when the shadow lifts and the mood swings wide to the opposite pole.

For me, the hyper side is even harder to understand. It makes no sense why he did what he did. Or how he could think his act would impress his father with the "power" and "force" of art. I don't even know why Lucien thinks that it was art. It wasn't even his idea.

It makes me feel far away from him. It makes me feel like he hasn't come back. I miss him more than when he was gone, now, at this very moment, as I hold him tightly in my arms and the long blue shade of afternoon creeps slowly up the grass.

LXIII

Hi Tess,

Just checking in like I said I would. Hope you're not screwing anything up. Did Dad meet your little French guy yet? That would be the best, you know. Less stupid than the present course.

Let me know what's going on.

Bill

P.S. I'm working on getting Christmas leave.

LXIV

I have never been to the opera before, and I feel like a princess in a tale. My eyes rove over the circling tiers—the velvet drapes, a color like persimmon, as heavy and still as the golden balconies themselves—all the way up to the stained-glass cupola in the sky. We are in a special box in El Teatro Colón. There's Lucien, Wid, Esme, Kai, and me, and some people from France who Solange is in charge of hosting in her role as cultural attaché. She's been keeping Lucien close these days, and this invitation is one more way of keeping him safely at her side.

Lucien looks beautiful. He is wearing a tuxedo and he looks like someone in a film. There's a small brown weed in his button-hole. I've never seen Wid in a suit before, and he looks like a First Communion boy. Kai is wearing purple, striking with her dark red hair, and Esme looks like a long, white flame. I'm in a dress I bought just for tonight. I told my mom that Esme's dad had given us the tickets, compliments of his company, and she suggested I go buy something nice to wear. She probably felt that if she could have a ball gown made, I should have a new dress too.

I couldn't have told the truth to her. And now, of course, I can't let them meet Lucien; everything's too precarious. *Lucien's* too precarious. I'm hoping too that news of the fountain won't get around. That time will pass and the story will simply disappear. I can just imagine what Dad would say.

Anyway, my dress is really beautiful. It's blackish gray and strapless, with a sash that ties around my hips in a wonderful, drippy bow. My hair is up with some wispy straggles hanging down. When Lucien turns to look at me, I can feel his eyes, like fingers, running up my cool, bare neck.

The French people shift in their velvet chairs. One of them scans the theater with tiny jeweled binoculars, then murmurs something to Solange. Solange responds with a quiet laugh. Her thick brown hair falls forward, and she brushes it back behind her ear so a pear-shaped diamond glints with light. She is wearing the simplest of gowns, a "little black dress" with the hem let down. She looks serene and comfortable. It's nothing to her, going to the opera. I'm sure she comes here once a week with embassy guests and who knows who. She has dozens of gowns in her closet at home; Esme showed them to me once. Watching her now, chatting softly with her guests, pointing her rubied finger to something in the program notes, I think of my mother's ball gown hanging on my closet door. It suddenly seems exactly like a prom dress, and my mom—I hate myself for thinking it—like a sheltered little high school girl. She still won't show it to my dad. He'll probably buy her a corsage.

La Bohème is beautiful. The music is so passionate and the story reminds me of Lucien. He holds my hand, but his eyes are closed. Sometimes he seems to wince in pain like he does when we're making love. At intermission we sit in a wonderful, crowded bar. It looks like a painting by Renoir—the flush-faced women, the black-tied men, glasses glittering in the air. We drink champagne and one of the French men tries to smoke. Solange has to tell him it's not allowed, and laughs when he says he thought there were more liberties in the "Paris of South America." Lucien translates this for me. Solange turns slowly as he speaks. Her smile is like a beam of sun.

"I love your dress," she tells me. "I've been looking at it all night long."

"Thank you," I say. I feel like I'm going to float away.

"Do you like the opera?"

"It's beautiful. I never knew—I feel as if—well, someone should have let me know." I sound like a perfect idiot, but Lucien's mother doesn't laugh.

"It's better like this—to discover it by yourself." She sips her drink, and after Lucien turns away and starts to talk to Wid: "I'm sorry I didn't respond to you when you sent that frantic email, Tess. I didn't know what to tell you then."

"I just wanted to know he was all right."

"But he wasn't all right. Do you know what he did?" I glance across the table. Wid is still talking to Lucien.

"Yes," I tell her. "I know what he did."

"He does things like that when . . . he gets upset. When my father died, his grandfather—"

"I know that, too. He told me. I know how much he loved him."

"You must be very special, Tess. He doesn't share his feelings much." There is something so soft about her face. She seems so full of interest, speaking in perfect English, switching to French when one of her guests addresses her, then gently turning back to me. "I hope that you will come to me. Talk to me, Tess, if something seems wrong. If Lucien doesn't—"

Lucien snaps from across the way. "Do stop gossiping, *Maman*!" His dark eyes flash between us, then pinpoint back on her.

"We aren't gossiping, are we, Tess? I was telling her how nice she looks. How very much I like her dress." She murmurs something else in French, and switches to lilting Spanish as someone she knows goes drifting by.

She's so charming and so elegant. So cordial to everybody there, to Lucien's friends and her group of guests, yet there's something quiet in her eyes, something like a veil. My mind runs back to the painting of her in Lucien's book with her bright red lips and the matching purse, and I think she's very different now. Something that was there is gone. A flurry of bells played on a silver xylophone announces intermission's end.

As we walk through the hallways back to our seats, Lucien whispers in my ear. "Please don't listen to *Maman*." He kisses my cheek and adds, *"Je t'aime."*

"I love you too," I answer. "And I love this night. It's beautiful." His clasp on my hand suddenly electrifies. I spin around and see him looking backward, down through the dark from where we've come.

"That's *him*!" he says in a whispered rasp. "That's him again! He was looking at you. I think he took your photograph."

"Where?"

"Right there. Going in through the door!" I turn around to the entrance of the orchestra, and my breath stands still at the back of my throat.

LXV

I t's Jerry. Jer. My dad's little dweeb assistant. Staring bluntly into my face with his blue and beady eyes. He lifts his cell phone for me to see, then stows it in his pocket and ushers his mother through the door. I turn away and hook my arm through Lucien's. I can't even talk. I can hardly breathe.

"You know him, Tess?" He pulls us forward toward the stairs. I'm shaking so hard, I have to clasp the handrail. I don't know if I'm more enraged or scared. Back in our box, I sit and try to collect myself.

"He works for my dad," I whisper.

"I've seen him before, I told you, Tess. That guy is following you around."

"Are you sure it's him?"

"I'm sure."

"And you're sure he took my photograph?"

"You saw him yourself, showing the phone. He wanted you to know he did."

"He was at the Marine House party too—I never told you, but he was."

"He was there when—"

"Don't even think of that," I breathe. "He didn't see us, he couldn't have."

"Would your father ask him to follow us?"

"Why would my father waste his time? If he thought that I was with you, he'd just—he doesn't need Jerry to spy for him."

"So what's the point?" asks Lucien.

"I don't know. He used to have some ministry, saving troubled kids. He seems to think it's still his job."

"We're not troubled, you and I."

"I think he knows I'm not supposed to be seeing you."

"But why does he care, this Jerry man?"

"I'm not sure. He might want to make my dad look bad. Show him how clueless he really is."

"And when he does, what will your father do to me?"

"Nothing," I say. Which is totally true. It's me, not him, who'll be faced with Dad. My stomach sinks as I think of that.

I cry in act four of *La Bohème*. I cry because it's horribly sad when Mimi dies, but I'm also crying for myself. It's so unfair that Jerry has ruined my perfect night. I wonder where he's sitting and if he's been watching all along, pinning me like a target in the orb of his binoculars. I wonder where else he's followed me, what else he knows about my life. I'm dizzy as we shuffle from the theater, shoulder to shoulder in the crowd. I lower my eyes and keep them down. I don't want to see his face again.

LXVI

I wish I could talk to Noree and tell her what's going on. Noree's so smart and sensible; she sees things with the clearest eyes. But I feel so weird about her and Mike and I don't know what to say. So instead I just imagine it. I imagine describing Jer to her and asking her what to do. I picture her face as she finds out that he's stalking us. And inside my head, I hear exactly what she says. I know she's right; she's always right, and that's how I know what I'm going to do: I'm going to tell my mom.

I'm going to tell the actual truth. That Lucien's mother, not Esme's dad, invited us to the opera. That I lied because I wanted to go so very much. I'm going to tell her that Jerry was spying on us there and at intermission took a picture with his phone. I'm going to tell her how much I love opera and Lucien and how tired I am of always lying and sneaking around.

On Sunday at church I plan my speech. In my mind I practice what I'll say. I have the strangest feeling that she'll listen and won't be mad at me. I have a feeling she'll understand. She'll be freaked out by Jerry too, I think. It was one thing for him to watch us while Dad was out of town, but she'll find it weird and creepy for him to be following me around. But when I go out to the patio, where she always hangs out on Sundays, I see that Dad is also there.

They're both stretched out on side-by-side chaise lounges, and I notice that they're holding hands. There are pale green drinks on the flagstones in between their chairs.

"Tess!" greets Mom as I'm just about to slip away. She pushes up higher in the chair. She's wearing a yellow bathing suit with a flowered sarong tied over it.

For half a second I think about talking to both of them. A cozy talk, like kids and parents on TV have. But Dad's dark shades are filled with sky, and the sky is as hard as glass. He's shirtless, and again I notice his early tan. The hairs on his chest are reddish, tinted slightly in the sun. I follow his arm down to the hand that clasps Mom's frailer, paler hand. It's her wedding ring hand, and the small round diamond glitters there. Something feels strange, but I can't say what. Maybe I don't want to know. Dad's been around a lot these days, and Mom's been happy, I can tell. There's a kind of heat hovering around their chairs.

"You should go for a swim," Mom tells me now. "The water's really nice." The pool is blue and the ripples on top are bright with sun. But I sure don't want to go for a swim with the two of them sitting there holding hands. And forget about talking to either one. What was I thinking anyway?

Tyler's out with Sam today, so Smoky follows me to my room. We sit on my bed and I try to draw her picture. But she won't sit still, and I finally give up. Lucien is at some function with Solange, which means I can't even text with him.

I think again of Noree. Sunday in December: She's probably at some football game cheering her head off for Mike. Afterward, they'll all go off to the sports bar/pizza place near school. Smoky knows that I feel like hell and tries to make me play with her. There's nothing here to play with, so I amble down to Tyler's room.

The walls of Tyler's room are white, and they're very bright with sun. On one of the walls is a poster of a golden retriever playing with a kitten. On another wall hangs a great big *T* that hung on his door in Annandale. His computer sits on a new white desk with built-in bookshelves overhead. Most of the books have something to do with World War II and his other favorite subject: dogs. There is dog stuff all around the place. His light brown bedspread is patterned with a paw print, Dalmatian pillows piled on top. There are two stuffed dogs resting in the pillow mounds. On the floor there's a furry dog bed, which is used for storing Smoky's toys. I grab a fuzzy squirrel with a squeaky thing inside its tail, and Smoky starts jumping up and down. I throw and she fetches, like fifty times, as if it's the greatest fun on earth.

After a while I pull out a different toy. As I throw it around I start to think that the dog toys look like baby toys. And then I think that there's too much furry stuff in here—even Tyler's slippers, peeking out from under the bed, have a doggy face and ears—and that maybe something's wrong. Like Tyler's in need of cuddling. No one cuddles him anymore, so he cuddles himself in fur. The thought makes me really sad. And it makes me love Smoky even more; that dog has been doing a very big job. I'm going to help her, I tell myself. I'm going to play with Tyler more. Tell stories and stuff like I used to do before everything got so crazy here.

LXVII

In art class we are working in pairs, doing portraits of each other. We sit at the tables face-to-face, and a lot of the students find this strange. Their nervous laughter fills the room. For Lucien and me, it's as natural as breathing to stare into each other's eyes. Yet I've never actually drawn his face. Only now do I really and truly look at it and see what makes it as it is.

I start at one dark, curved eyebrow, which forms the top of the crescent shape that runs above his eye. I see how the shape meets the bridge of the nose. How the base of the nose ends at the midpoint of the eye. How the mouth extends beyond the rounding of the nose where the shadowy nostril is encased.

I finally draw those soft, deep dents I always seem to think about—that place where the mouth, curvy and full, cuts blurry commas in the flesh. I forget who I am drawing and lose myself in the pleasure of the flowing shapes, the slopes and swirls that have no name or meaning now other than how they look.

"Beautiful!" Pasacalia yelps. Her voice makes me jump, and the pencil skids, leaving a long gray mark. "That's a very accomplished drawing, Tess." She glances over at Lucien's book. "The idea was to work together. While Tess draws you, you draw Tess."

"Sorry," Lucien says to her as she clicks her tongue and moves away to look at the other students' work. "Let me see," he urges, craning toward my book. I slowly turn it for him to view, and still looking down, he murmurs, "Am I really that beautiful to you?"

"I drew what I saw. Stop talking and show me what you've done." He flips his sketchbook around to me. The page is nearly empty. There are six or seven shaky lines. And an oval that might suggest my eye.

"I can't draw anymore," he tells me. "Something happened to me in France."

"What do you mean?"

"I don't know. I just can't draw since I've been back."

"Why?"

"I don't know."

"But that makes no sense."

"Something's blocked."

"It will come back."

But Lucien says it will never come back. That something inside's been flattened. Broken, damaged, completely lost.

LXVIII

I have this idea. It comes to me in bed that night. We should go out sketching, Lucien and I, like he and his *grand-père* used to do. For a while I can't sleep. I'm so excited thinking of this; I know that it will help him and get him back into doing his art.

The next day when I tell him, he says that he will try. I work at the Casa that afternoon, but after school the following day we go to La Boca planning to draw. La Boca, "the mouth," is a seedy portside neighborhood famous for its brightly painted buildings and the artwork sold along the streets. Most of the art is awful—tango dancers and garish portraits of Carlos Gardel— but it's fun to walk around the place. There are lots of tourists milling about, snapping pictures as they go. They pose in front of the bright facades, on splashes of yellow and turquoise blue, on the rectangle of a bright red door.

We stop for *café dobles* at a table near the waterfront. Here the color is monotone. Rusty barges and shabby boats sit motionless at the run-down dock, and around our feet a bunch of lazy dogs are splayed.

"We should have come here," I say with a smile, "to get a dog for Tyler." I look at one of the filthy mutts. "He's ugly enough to be his type." Lucien smiles. He knows all about Tyler and his dogs.

"Once Wid tried to take one home, but the dog ran away and came back here. They like the street. They're gypsy dogs. Anyway, doesn't Tyler like his dog?"

I laugh at that. "'Like' is not the word for it. He'd marry his dog if the two of them weren't underage."

"Me too," says Lucien under his breath. He's gazing out at the flat, gray water beyond the docks. "I'd marry you too and run away. I'd take you to France. To the countryside where *Grand-père* had his house."

His words make me feel unbalanced—a sort of all-body dizziness, and I turn to find his eyes. "You really think about things like that?"

"Why not? Don't you?"

"I think of them all the time. I imagine whole scenes and stories. Sometimes I see it like a film—the two of us in pictures. Walking along the Seine and stuff."

Lucien smiles. "Do you ever imagine that we could have a baby?"

A flush of heat ripples through my body. I can't believe he's asking this, and it makes me feel shaky deep inside. "If we did," I say in the quietest voice, "I'd want it to be a boy. With curly blond hair just like yours."

"I'd rather have a baby girl. A tiny girl who looks like you."

He moves from his chair and comes to hold me from behind, his arms around my shoulders, his face against my hair. "You'd look beautiful fat and pregnant. I'd feed you fruit and pudding and serve you breakfast in the bed."

"Pudding?"

"Oh, yes. Chocolate and banana. Pudding with cream and yellow peaches on the top." He kisses my hair and holds me very tight. I can feel him trembling slightly, his fingers clenched at the top of my arms.

We do no drawings that afternoon.

LXIX

On Thursday afternoon we go to the Japanese Gardens. The air is warm and the flowers are all in bloom. Monet would have loved to paint this place. We walk for a while, then sit on a bench near one of the arching bridges. Its shape makes me think of the contour under Lucien's brow.

I take out my paints and contemplate the shining pond. Its edge is pink with the bright reflection of blossoming trees. The pink forms a frilly scallop against the city buildings, flat and geometric, rising to the sky. Lucien has gone to sit near the edge of the pond. I think he's started to sketch the carp—overgrown goldfish with swishy tails—that jostle near the bank to feed.

The day is still and windless. It's pleasant to sit in the sun and paint, though I have to work fast and spray the paper to keep it wet; the color dries in the brilliant light the moment I sweep it on. I like how impromptu my painting looks, and I leave some parts unfinished—some empty space where the sky might be. I date it and sign my name below.

Lucien's page is a flurry of spiky, twisted lines. *Poissons Rouges*, he's scrawled in orange over the spikes.

LXX

I almost freak out when I learn that it is Chatter Night. It's Tyler who actually lets me know, running to greet me at the gate, Smoky close behind. "A general's coming tonight!" he yells. "Smoky's gonna play dead for him."

"Shit," I say, not meaning to. "No one told me it was tonight." If I had known I would have for sure made other plans. I have to think fast. Like, on the spot. If Jer is coming, I can't be here. I almost turn around and run, but right at that moment my mom appears from the side of the house, some just-picked flowers in her arms.

"Hi there, Tess. Look at these delphinium! Aren't they incredible?" Her hair is slightly tousled and her face is flushed from working in the sun.

"I didn't know it was Chatter Night."

"I guess I forgot to mention it." She shakes her hair and shifts the flowers into one arm. "Come on in. I want you to see my shoes for the ball."

A flash of irritation snaps; I'm tired of hearing about her ball. It's all she seems to think about, and it seems so trite and stupid with everything else that's going on. With me, I mean—and Lucien. With what's happening to Lucien.

Inside the house everything's set for Chatter Night. There's the smell of lemon oil and wax. The cocktail napkins in their piles. In the kitchen, Nidia is setting out glasses on a tray. The pigs-in-blankets are all arranged, and I'm sure if I look in that steaming pot I'll find the baby hot dogs in the horrible jam-and-mustard sauce. I say hello to Nidia as she takes the flowers from my mom. She leans to inhale the smell of them, eyes half closed, the pleasure dreamy on her face.

"Come on, Tess," Mom says to me. She really wants me to see her shoes. I follow her up the stairway and down the hall to my parents' room. I realize as I step inside that I hardly ever come here. I almost feel like I've never actually seen this place.

Everything's done in blue and white, like one of those china dinner plates. It's nothing like Solange's room, with its giant paintings on the wall and the bed with its posts of eland horn. You can tell which section is hers or Dad's. His bureau is tall and hers is low. She has family pictures on top of hers and Dad has a dish of coins. His mirror is small and hers is big. She also has a vanity with a basket of makeup on the top and a little Lenox china clock.

The shoes are in a pale blue box. She takes a breath before slowly opening the lid. "What do you think?" she asks me. Like she's the girl and I'm the mom.

The shoes are a sort of greenish blue. Satin with a low heel. A gathered bow with a diamond stud. For a minute I think I'm going to cry. Pictures are racing through my mind—crazy snapshots of Lucien's mother's elegant shoes on the floor of her open closet, in the see-through slots of shoe bags hanging on the doors. She'd never own tacky shoes like this. I look at my mom, at the hushed excitement on her face.

"Wow," I say. "They're beautiful."

Dad doesn't know what to make of me. I'm wearing a skirt I meant to throw out and a shirt that belongs to Mom.

"What a pretty blouse," says Mrs. McKnight as I pass the cream-cheese roll-up snacks. Smoky has just played dead to a round of huge applause, and General Tooms has pinned a medal on Tyler's chest. Tyler looks about to burst. I hope he knows that Tooms will want it back again. I've been doing the rounds for half an hour, smiling and making small talk; the ache in my face goes ear to ear.

Jer, all the while, is playing cat-and-mouse with me. He's said hello and has taken two hors d'oeuvres. He hasn't eaten either one; he thinks that I don't see them side by side behind the lamp. I try to latch on to Tyler so Jer can't be with me alone, but Tyler's showing off his medal and the female guests are fussing like crazy over him. Sometimes he's so goddamn cute.

I glance at my watch. Two more minutes and I am done. I gather some crumpled napkins and head for the kitchen with my tray. I'm right at the door, my hand is actually *on* the door, when Jer slinks up behind me. All I have to do is push; it's the simplest kind of swinging door and beyond it there is Nidia and the safety of the kitchen where guests don't go as if by law. But I freeze in place at the sound of his voice. It's like I've just gone paralyzed.

LXXI

Jerry takes the tray from me. I watch it slide from my useless hands. I want to bolt but I just can't move. I'm totally immobilized.

"Tessa," he says. "You're playing with fire."

That's hilarious, I know. I mean, part of me hears what a giant, dumb cliché that is, but another part thinks how crazy Jerry has to be, how absolutely whack he is. Next he says, "Look at me, Tess."

I still don't move, and I certainly don't look at him. Not at his face, at any rate; instead I stare at a place at the bottom of his neck. There are clumps of black and grayish hair, and vaguely I think that the hair must be coming from his chest—that hair doesn't really grow on necks—and the hairs must be seven inches long. There's a ruby stud on his golden cross.

"Listen, Tess, I'm on your side, I want you to know."

On my side? Now I'm really getting scared. I take a breath; I'm going to run. Not to the kitchen—the other way. Right around him and up the stairs.

But then he says "Lucien du Previn" and my eyes leap to his face. "Good," he says. "Keep looking there." He points a finger at his eyes. They're small and blue; you can tell he thinks they're very intense, especially now, with his finger aiming into them.

"I think you know he's trouble, Tess." He narrows his gaze and does something clenchy to his jaw. It's the same thing Dad has started to do. "He was recently arrested for vandalizing an important monument in Rome. This wasn't his first destructive act. He has a record in France, as well. In addition to that, he's been hospitalized for mental instability. The boy is manic-depressive, Tess."

I'm dumbstruck still, but a part of my mind is waking up. I know it's better not to talk. *Don't volunteer anything,* Dad always says. So I don't tell Jer that I know all this. I just stand there and let the wacko talk.

"If he were just bipolar, another term for what he has, without displays of criminal behavior, I wouldn't make a case of this. But vandalism—destructive acts of any kind, especially when they escalate—are big red flags one can't ignore." He takes a breath and lowers his voice. "I don't want to scare you, Tessa, but the violence he does to objects could someday turn on you."

"What?" I don't want to talk, but the word comes springing out of my mouth.

"Try to stay calm," says Jerry. He thinks I'm scared of Lucien instead of scared of him. "I know you're fond of du Previn. Maybe you think you love him. But I also know that deep inside, you know that there's a problem. That's why you choose to sneak around."

"What do you want?" I finally ask. My voice is quivery and weak, and drops of sweat are trickling down behind my knees. Jer's still holding the hors d'oeuvres tray, yet he gestures with his other hand, turning up his palm.

"I want you to be safe," he says.

"What?"

"I want you to be safe—that's it. I'm your father's assistant. It's my job."

"It's not your—"

"Your father's very busy. He doesn't have time to follow every single lead—"

"What 'lead'?" I rasp. "This isn't a case—there is no *lead*."

"I haven't told him anything yet, but if you want I'll give him all the data. The record of the arrest in Rome. The medical info, the—"

"That's private information. How did you even—"

"I made it my business. It's easy stuff." I remember laughing with my mom about Jerry getting all gung ho. It doesn't seem very funny now.

"I still don't know what you want from me."

"I want you to stay away from him."

"Why do you care?"

"It's who I am." Jerry gives a helpless shrug. "If I see a person walking into danger and I don't do my best to stop her, I feel like I'm slacking on my job. That's what I have always done: I keep folks out of danger, Tess."

"You know, Dad doesn't like when you do this stuff." I stop and take a shallow breath. "He doesn't like when you go exploring on your own." Jerry blinks. He hardly has a poker face. "I heard my dad telling someone on the phone. It might have been someone from Washington." I'm making this up as I go along, and I think I'm doing pretty good when he suddenly starts to laugh. It's a phony laugh, and it really sets my nerves on edge.

"I also heard him on the phone. Maybe two months back— he was talking to his sister, Kate. I believe that he had grounded you. He was taking off for Paraguay." He stops for a moment. Nods his head like some distant memory's creeping back. "I distinctly heard him tell her that he might have to ship you off to her—if you didn't start toeing the line, that is, with regard to a certain boy."

Now it's Jer who's hit a nerve. I try not to show it in my face, but I feel a tremor in my jaw. I wonder if what he's said is true. Dad was pretty awful then. He might have considered sending me home. And if Jer hadn't heard Dad talking, how would he even know about Kate?

"Do you really think," says Jerry then, "that your father would be upset with me for keeping you out of danger—for finding the truth about this boy?" He isn't blinking anymore; he's staring flatly into my face, and both of us know he's won. "Really, Tessa, what do you think?"

"Why can't you just leave me alone?" My voice is squeaky along the edge. "Don't you have other things to do?"

"I have a lot of things to do. So I wish you'd just cooperate.

Plus, don't you kind of like it here? I'm sure Aunt Kate is really nice, but life is good for an embassy kid. Do you really want to go back home?"

I don't know what to say to him. *I'm not going home* is all I can think. *No one can make me go back home.* I look into Jerry's beady eyes. It's crazy, the fantasy I have. I'm suddenly leaping forward, grabbing for his leg. I clasp the gun and yank it from the holster—that khaki bulge on the side of his leg—and shoot him in the head. The thought of it makes me dizzy, and I lean my back against the wall.

"It's over," I finally say to him. "The night at the opera was it for us." There's a little flutter in his eyes.

"On the level?"

"Yes." I try to sound sad and serious. I'm totally *on the level*, Jer.

I'll teach you how to do it, Lucien once said to me. *How to lie so good that no one sees it in your eyes.*

I think I've learned. I think I'm there. Because Jerry is bobbing his head again, and there's something like a smile creeping across his face. "I'm really glad to hear that. I'm glad you finally figured it out." He pushes the tray back into my hands and turns around to the living room. He takes a few steps, then adds like it's an afterthought: "Honestly, Tess, I'd hate to see it happen. I'd hate to see you sent back home."

LXXII

We are in the huge walled cemetery in La Recoleta. It was Lucien's idea to come here to sketch the mausoleums. It's a cool, gray day; the rooftop angels, their wings spread wide, seem to hang in the low, dark sky. Already I've felt some drops of rain. We have turned off the main path and are winding our way through alleys of smaller mausoleums. The deeper we go into the stony labyrinth, the more desolate it gets. The walks are cracked and broken, and weeds spring up through the tilted stones. The mausoleums too are damaged and untended with broken windows and gaping doors, their dark interiors filled with leaves. The air is thick with the smell of cats. Hundreds of them live here. They bask on the slabs of marble and slink like ghosts between the small, bleak houses and the clumps of creeping juniper.

Lucien and I pick out a mausoleum we like. It is stained and faintly green with moss. The glass of the ironwork door is cracked, and the windows are furred with spiderwebs. On a shelf inside lie stalks of long-dead flowers and a rotted strand of rosary beads. Lucien lays his raincoat down and we sit and take our sketchbooks out. I've been waiting all day for a quiet time to talk to him. I start to trace the iron curlicues on the door.

"My dad's assistant was over at my house last night." His eyelids flicker quickly, but aside from that he doesn't move. "He told me to stay away from you or he'll tell my dad some stuff he knows."

"Stuff?"

"About you."

"Like what?"

"He said he knows what you did in Rome. And he knows about things you did in France—probably when your *grand-père*—"

"How the hell could he know all that?"

"I don't know, but he said he does. He also said . . ." I try to even out my voice. "He said you'd been in the hospital—" I hear the sound as he catches his breath and flashes around to look at me. His face is pale and stunned.

"Listen, Lucien, I don't care. I just wanted you to know."

"It isn't true," he says in a kind of whispered shout. "It isn't true what they say I am. I was sad when *Grand-père* died—that's all."

"I told you, Lucien, I don't care."

"But *I* care, Tess. I am not crazy. I was sad."

"No one said 'crazy,' Lucien."

"Manic-depressive, what is that? It's a crazy way that people are, and I am not that way." He is shaking his head from side to side, soundlessly mouthing "no." Then whispering fiercely

WHEN YOU OPEN YOUR EYES

between his teeth: "*Thees* man is crazy. I am not. Why is he pursuing us? Why is he so obsessed with us?"

"I don't know. He says it's his job to keep me out of danger. He's like a Boy Scout hooked on speed."

"He's a little Napoleon," Lucien says. "He wants to control the world."

"He told me that a few months back he heard my dad talking to his sister. He said that Dad was thinking of sending me off to her. She lives in Virginia, not far from us. Jerry kept hinting that if he ratted me out to Dad, that's where I'd end up."

"Would your mother let him send you back?"

"I don't know. On Sunday I almost talked to her. I went out in the yard to find her, but my dad was there, and I just had the feeling . . . I don't know. I only wanted to tell my mom."

"Maybe I should tell *Maman*." Lucien mulls this over. "But then, of course, it would lead her to your father and everything would end the same."

We sink into silence for a while. He starts to make squiggles on the page. It's raining very slightly now; it's hardly more than mist. "Maybe, Tess," he says, still looking at his book, "if I were not so selfish, I'd simply let you go. Life would be easy for you then."

"That isn't true. My life would be unbearable." He drops the pencil from his hand and throws his sketchbook onto the ground. His eyes are dark and liquidy. He climbs to his feet and moves to the door of the mausoleum. It creaks on the hinge as he opens it, making a crack for us to pass. Dried-up leaves form crinkly piles in the corners of the floor. The cobwebs are glittery with rain. As I step inside I can smell the dampness of the place, the mold and moss and air that's never touched by sun.

Lucien throws his raincoat down. He closes the door and we sink to the floor. He covers me with his body, and his warmth seeps slowly into my bones.

"In Venice," he whispers into my ear, "there's a cemetery island. Isola di San Michele. I went there once and walked for hours. I found a place where they buried Russian princesses." He's touching the zipper of my jeans, and I feel his hand against my skin. "Venice had been so crowded, and there it was so peaceful. I felt as if I could hear the people whispering."

"And you weren't scared?" My body trembles under his hand.

"No," he murmurs into my ear. "It made me feel like everything's eternal." He kisses my neck and drags his mouth to the pit of my throat. "Are we eternal?"

"What?"

"Are we eternal, you and I? Will we go on forever, Tess?"

"Yes," I say through my indrawn breath. He raises himself and I know what he is doing. His hands are low and fumbling and he's suddenly panting very hard.

"Tess," he murmurs through his breaths, "I want you to have my baby. I want for it to happen now."

I open my eyes. I feel like I'm waking from a dream. From the mossy ceiling an ornate lantern hangs from a chain, each tiny pane a dark and dusty octagon. A breath of mold seeps into my lungs, and I suddenly realize where I am. I am in a grave. I am in a tomb. And Lucien, above me—I don't know where he is at all.

I press my hands against the floor, and with all my strength, jerk my body away and back. I twist my hips and pull myself free of Lucien. I can hardly breathe. I'm terrified. I don't know how I got here—here, I mean, to this dark, cold place, this space of death, where I don't remember who I am.

I zip my clothes and crawl like a crab from the mausoleum. It's raining for real, and I'm glad for that. I throw back my head so the cold, clean water can wash my face. I pick up Lucien's sketchbook from where it's floating in the rain-soaked weeds. The pages are filled with nothing. Random scribbles. Jittery scrawls.

Drawings, Lucien said one day, are more intense than photographs. They're the actual lines the person has made with the impulse of his nerves and touch. Lucien's lines are broken. They look like twigs torn and scattered in a storm.

LXXIII

Hi Tess,

Just checking in. Hope everything's fine and you're using your head. Maybe by now Mom and Dad have met your Frenchie and everything's good. That's what I'm hoping, anyway, since I haven't heard any news from u. I saw a picture of Tyler's dog. Talk about a mutt. How's the artwork going? Meet anyone new at school? Let me know what's happening. As for me, since you're so concerned, it's been hot as hell the last few days. We're busy building toilets. I don't think you'd enjoy it much.

Your big bro, Bill

P.S. Not totally sure about Christmas yet.

LXXIV

Lucien's started to wear a hat. It's more like a skullcap really, knitted and black, stretchy enough to hold his curls. He says I should also be disguised. I like to think that Jer believes we've broken up, but Lucien says he's crazy and is probably secretly on our tail.

He looks so different in his hat. His face looks stark without his curls, and his eyes seem very big. I hardly ever look at his mouth, which I used to stare at all the time. Maybe the drugs his doctor in France prescribed for him do something to his eyes; they seem so still and almost black.

He isn't angry anymore. He says I was right to stop him in the mausoleum. It was crazy to think that we could have a baby. That we could run away to France. Live happily ever after there. We don't go sketching anymore. That day was the last. The end of that. We haven't made love—or tried to—since that rainy afternoon.

The good news is, he has finally started to draw again. He is working on a project, something secret he's doing at home, and very soon he will let me see.

LXXV

We get the big news that Bill's coming home for Christmas. He'll stay with us for a couple of weeks and in January go back to finish his sophomore year. Tyler's thrilled that he's coming back and is teaching Smoky a whole new repertoire of tricks. Dad suggests that we go away for Christmas to Bariloche in the south, which I've heard looks just like Switzerland, but Mom really wants to stay at home and have the Christmas we always have. I really don't care if we stay or go. It's Jerry I wish would take a trip.

The Marine Ball is a week away. My mom and her friends have arranged for people to come to our house that afternoon to do their hair and nails. That's nice, I guess. Like something Noree and I would do. Or would have done, whatever. I don't want to think of Noree. It makes me too sad, and I'm sad enough.

In the meantime, the ball gown hangs on my closet door. I stare at it a lot. I don't know why, but it seems so full of meaning. It looks so innocent hanging there.

LXXVI

At last I see the drawings. Lucien brings them into school and lays them out on the art room floor. There are twelve in all, each depicting a strange and beautifully rendered box. Each box is adorned with details—cord and bindings and tangled wires. Some have parcels tied on top, tiny bags and pouches that somehow look Japanese. They are numbered, and underneath are messages in a secret code that only Lucien can read. Mrs. Pasacalia stands there, staring down at them. Her face is very grim.

"Are these what I think they are?" she says.

Lucien smiles. "I don't know."

"They look to me like IEDs. I've seen some photographs online."

"As beautiful as these?" he asks.

"I'm not sure I'd call them beautiful."

"You don't like my drawings?"

"I don't like the theme."

I turn from Pasacalia and look at the drawings at our feet.

I had no idea what they were before. Improvised Explosive Devices. He's drawn a series of beautiful bombs.

"Why would you choose a subject like this?" Pasacalia asks him next. "You don't do any work for weeks and suddenly you fix on this?" I'm starting to think she's heard about the fountain and that's why she's fallen out of love.

"I think they're interesting," Lucien says. "They're like found art—made with scraps of this and that."

"It's not a pleasant subject. There are millions of other things to draw." She turns her frowning gaze at me. "Have you seen these, Tess? Does the subject offend you the slightest bit—I mean, as an American?"

I don't know what to say to her. I'm still absorbing the whole idea—the mystery of the boxes, the care with which he's rendered them, and the fact that he's started to draw again. I'm not quite sure why she's so upset.

"Tess?" she repeats, her eyebrow raised. "Take a good look at what these are."

"They don't offend me," I answer her. "Weapons can be beautiful. Spanish daggers. Medieval swords. Have you ever seen—"

"Those weapons are ancient artifacts. These are depictions of weapons being used today—by terrorists around the world. They don't deserve to be glorified." Pasacalia pauses. "Lucien, Tess, I loved your circle project. It was fun and so original. But this—well, this could be misconstrued." She moves toward the door and turns to add in her best, most sober teacher voice:

"Don't defend this, Tessa. Be your own person; think for yourself. And both of you, I don't want these drawings in the school."

"That means they're good," says Lucien as we kneel on the floor to gather them up. "I never meant them to be 'fun.' That's not the point of guerilla art."

I'm still burning up over what Pasacalia said to me—*Be your own person; think for yourself*—as if she thinks I'm under Lucien's control. It reminds me of my parents and makes me want to scream.

Strangely, it's the drawings that manage to calm me down. When I see them up close, I'm struck by how delicate they are, how detailed and meticulous. Each wire is so precisely drawn. Each hanging pouch, which I realize now is full of nails or shards of glass, is drafted with exquisite care. They make me think of still lifes—gorgeously rendered cups and spoons, a light-struck drop on a goblet's lip.

"They're beautiful," I tell him. "And part of what makes them beautiful is the dangerous function they suggest. The beauty is ironical. And that's what she's too dumb to see."

"*Oui,*" he says as he binds the drawings into his portfolio. "Things that kill are often very beautiful. Italian cup-hilt rapiers. Dueling pistols. English swords. Even the red Swiss Army knife with its shiny little claws."

It's five o'clock and the room is full of shadows. Almost everyone has left the school except for the last few janitors pushing their quiet mops.

"I bought something for you," he tells me when we finish

wrapping up his work. From his pocket he pulls a long red, clip-on ponytail. I laugh when I see it.

"It doesn't even match my hair."

That's why he chose it, he explains. He gives me a bandanna next. It's one of those calico cowboy scarves, red with black and white designs.

"First you clip the hair on. Then over it you wear the scarf. You'll look completely different, Tess." There's a mirror in the art room and I stand there to clip the ponytail and tie the cotton scarf. I smile at Lucien in the glass, but he doesn't smile back.

As we leave the school, he glances up and down the street. Raises the collar of his shirt. He walks me only halfway home to the corner of my block. I think that he will kiss me, but then I remember that he won't.

"Be careful," he says. "The air has eyes."

LXXVII

Tuesday. Esme drags Lucien, Kai, and me to help her shop for her Venice trip. Kai says it's disgusting—the whole idea of her and Gash—but comes along with us anyway.

Avenida Sante Fe is bustling as always, the traffic so loud we can hardly talk. Esme stops at a small, expensive-looking store. A woman in black and a string of pearls ushers us in and locks the door, abruptly shutting out the noise. It's strange to look back through the tinted glass and see the world still rushing by like a silent sequence in a film. Esme buys a winter coat and a Russian-style hat.

It's cold in Venice now, she says. Lucien says it snowed one time when he was there and that Esme should come home with him and steal a pair of boots. Kai and I trade glances. No one's been at Lucien's since he came back from France, and the reason for going now is strange. He used to hate when Esme raided his mother's realm.

When we get to the apartment, he unlocks the door and flings it open with so much force that the doorknob chips the wall. The apartment is still, and we enter like invaders, Lucien the leader, motioning us to follow him. We reach Solange's bedroom and he stomps his way inside. He throws both doors of the closet wide so it gapes like a startled mouth.

"Take whatever you want," he says. "I think the boots are toward the back." Kai and I just stand there as Esme dives into the wall of clothes. There are dresses and suits and blouses, and sleek, dark gowns in their plastic bags. On the back of the door a bathrobe and a nightgown hang. The nightgown is long, of ivory silk with a faint design of leaves. From the way it's hung, just looped on a hook, I can tell she wore it to bed last night. Down on the floor is a pair of ivory slippers toppled on their sides. There's a scent in the air, a scent that's hers, and now that I feel I know her, it doesn't seem right to be rummaging through her clothes.

Esme is on her hands and knees, crawling through the silky hems to reach the stash of boots in back. I turn to look at Lucien and his face is strange, unreadable. Yet I somehow feel the ugly picture pleases him—the sight of Esme on the floor, rooting through his mother's things.

LXXVIII

The following day Lucien is not in school. I call and leave him messages, but he doesn't answer back. I'm tired of the pattern, and I don't want to go through this again. Part of me thinks I should let him brood—give him time to be alone. But my other part is frightened. He was strange at his apartment. I'd never seen him act like that—angry and stomping, slamming doors, barging into his mother's room. I'm scared about his changing moods, and the way he's drifting off again to that isolated place.

I call five times on Thursday and again I do not hear from him. I take some OxyContin from the slot inside my purse—not even a half, just a tiny nibble off the edge.

In with the pills, I see the slip of paper where Paul wrote his telephone number down. I take it out and stare at it, and for just the briefest second my mind runs off, remembering. I see him as he looked that night: muscled, tall, and handsome, running out from the restaurant calling my name.

Then I think: What if I had answered him? A twinge of guilt

ripples through my stomach, and I crumple the slip of paper and throw it on the floor. I put on my long red ponytail. I take the train into Retiro Station and make my way to Lucien's.

From down on the street in front his apartment, I send a text and tell him where I am. I go inside and ask the *portero* to ring him up. He's waiting when I get there, standing outside the apartment door.

"What's going on?" I try to sound firm, like I'm the one in charge, not him. "Nothing," he says. "I'm working." He's wearing a pair of drawstring pants and the black kimono I love so much. Everything is wrinkled and I know he wore it all to bed. His hair is wild and smells like sleep.

"Why didn't you answer my calls?" I ask.

"I'm sorry, Tess. I couldn't."

"But why?"

"Just couldn't. . . .You shouldn't be here."

"I was worried about you, Lucien."

"I'm all right."

"You don't look all right. Is anyone home? Can I come in?"

"No!" he snaps; it's almost a shout. Then softer, but still with urgency: "You can't come in here anymore."

"What do you mean?" I don't wait for him to answer. I take a step forward and push inside. I grab his arm, and he doesn't resist. He doesn't do much of anything. Just stands there staring past my eyes as I shut the door behind his back.

"Why have you been staying home?"

"I told you, Tess. I'm working."

"Working on what?"

"My project."

"I must have called you a hundred times."

"You shouldn't call me anymore."

"Lucien, don't say that! Please don't talk to me like that."

"I'm only doing it for you."

"Lucien, stop! I don't care if you have problems. I love you whatever way you are. I want to help you if I can."

"You—help me? That's funny. Of all the people. You."

"Are you trying to hurt me to make me leave?"

"I'm trying to *save* you, Tessa. I wish that you'd just go!" My stomach drops at the thought that flickers through my mind.

"Did my dad's assistant threaten you?" I see the ripple in his skin, a jitter of nerves along his jaw. He smiles faintly. An ugly smile.

"No," he says, and his voice is a snarl.

"He did, I can tell—"

"He didn't."

"You're lying to me."

"I'm not."

"Lucien, please—"

"If I show you my work, will you go away?" He takes my hand and pulls me down the narrow hall. That's how I know I'm trembling. And it's not just my hand; it's all of me.

LXXIX

The bedroom is dark, the shades drawn down. There is only a small white work light on a studio table against the wall. The air feels close, a smell of unwashed bed sheets and a tingling of chemicals. I catch my breath as I look at the bed. It's covered with small, strange boxes—his intricate drawings come to life. They're all lined up—mysterious bundles, taped and wired; pouches that bulge with nails and shards. Tied on top with reams of cord are ticking clocks and vials of colored liquid—yellow, blue, and queasy green. Long, frayed fuses trail from deep inside each box. For a moment I just stand there. In the absence of our voices, the sound of the ticking is very loud. Loud and strange and ominous.

"Lucien—God." I take a step back. "Are these things *bombs*?"

I feel his smile. "Do they look like bombs?"

"I don't know. Just tell me they're not."

"Tell me what they look like first." The ticking sound unsettles me. Every clock has a different pitch and cadence, and all together the noise is totally dizzying.

"All right," I say. "They look like bombs—like IEDs."

"That's all I want to know," he says. He picks one up and tosses it for me to catch. I grab it midair—instinctively. As if I know the box will explode if it hits the floor. It's heavy in my shaking hands. And it looks so real and lethal, plump with nails, bound in filigrees of wire. He reaches for another. Shows me the swirly Arab script he's painted on the side. "They're totally fake—or are they? Could anyone really tell?"

"What are you going to do with them?"

"I'm going to exhibit them."

"What do you mean?"

"Like our circle project. Put them around."

"But where?"

"That's the secret part," he says.

My eyes sweep over the bed again. "These aren't like the circles." I set down the box he's tossed to me and take another in my hands. Tied on top is a vial of yellow liquid; I don't want to think what it might be. "Lucien." I'm careful as I choose my words. "You can't just put these anywhere. People could think they're real."

"That's the whole idea of it."

"But Lucien . . . it's dangerous."

"Dangerous? Why? If they aren't real."

"It's dangerous to *you*, I mean. If someone sees you planting them, they might think you're—"

"But they'd be wrong, now wouldn't they? They would just be paranoid."

"But if people think—"

"I want them to think whatever they think. I *want* them to be paranoid. They make *us* paranoid, *n'est-ce pas*?"

"I know that Jerry threatened you. But please don't do this, Lucien. It's only going to make things worse."

"Jerry did not threaten me."

"Then what the hell is going on?"

Lucien grabs the box from me. "It's all about deception. They lie to us, so I lie to them."

"Who?"

"Just go! Do you hear me—go!" He suddenly grabs my arm again. Pulls me roughly toward the door. "You have to go. My mother will be coming home."

"I don't care if your mother comes home. She happens to like me, Lucien. That night at the opera she—"

"My mother doesn't know who you are."

"What is that supposed to mean?" His eyes, which up till now have avoided mine, finally meet my gaze. They're dark and still and glitter with a sheen of tears.

"I love you, Tess," he whispers. "But it's over and you have to go."

"Lucien, no!"

"You have to go." He takes my wrist in both his hands and pulls me through the door. He's stronger than I ever dreamed, and he drags me down the hallway and through the long red living room. I see the sky in the wall of glass. He opens the door and shoves me out. I don't even know I'm crying until he tells me, "Stop."

"No!" I scream. I struggle to push my way back in, but he shuts the door and I hear the clicking of the lock.

LXXX

I have to tell Solange. She asked me to be in touch with her if something seemed wrong with Lucien. I write her an email and say that I am worried. I tell her how he pushed me out and how crazy and depressed he seemed. I tell her about the IEDs and what he plans to do with them.

Solange responds the following day. She thanks me for being so concerned. He isn't well, she tells me, and cannot go to school right now. She's sorry he broke up with me and hopes that I'll be patient. These episodes sometimes last for weeks.

As for the "bombs," she says she checked; there are no strange boxes in his room. Maybe he dismantled them. He does that, she says, when he's tired of a project and feels there's nothing more to do. She thanks me again for my concern. And signs the note *Your friend, Solange.*

I'm sitting in the computer lab staring at her message when Kai and Esme come drifting in. I'm surprised to see them. I'd stayed to do some artwork, but they usually hurry out at three.

"I'm getting my hair dyed. Want to come?" Esme says in a sleepy voice.

"Say yes," says Kai. "We can do our nails." She rounds the desk and looks at the computer screen. "Any news from Lucien?"

"I heard from Solange," I tell her. Maybe because I feel alone, I let her read the email. She leans in close, screwing up her face as she reads the words.

Then, "Shit," she says. "Did you really break up?"

"He said it's over."

"Why?"

"I don't know. But something's really wrong with him. Yesterday I went to his apartment . . ." It's hard to talk, remembering.

"And?"

"He was really weird and told me I had to leave. He kept saying his mother was coming home."

"Maybe," says Kai, "she's sick of people rummaging through her stuff." She looks at Esme pointedly.

"All I took was a pair of boots. She doesn't even know they're gone."

Kai turns back to the screen again. "What's this stuff about bombs?" she asks.

I try to explain Lucien's latest project.

"I don't get it. What's the point?"

"They're *fake*," says Esme, slowly drawing out the word. "But they look so real. It's crazy. They have all these little bags on top and these test tubes full of—"

"You've *seen* them?" I yelp.

"Yeah, sort of."

"What do you mean?"

"They're at my place. He asked if he could store them there."

I can see Kai thinking as Esme talks, the frown lines deepening on her face.

"They're phony, right? But he wants them to look like actual bombs?" She looks from me to Esme. "What's he going to do with them?"

Esme shrugs. "Have fun with them."

"Fun?"

"They're totally fake."

"He's an idiot," Kai murmurs. Then, speaking straight at Esme, "Where is he going to have this 'fun'?"

"He made me promise not to tell."

"Who cares what he made you promise? Don't you see that he might get hurt?"

"How?" says Esme. "If they're fake?" Kai shakes her head like she can't believe that Esme's real.

"I don't know who's stupider, you or him. What if someone sees him? What if the police get called?" She lowers her voice. "You have to tell us, Esme. Where is he going to put these things?"

Esme seems genuinely confused. Like she can't imagine what could possibly go wrong.

I grab her shoulders with both my hands. "Where?" I rasp. "Just tell us where."

"He's mad at his mum," she murmurs.

"Where is he going to put those things?"

"If he asks, don't say I told you." I loosen my grip on Esme. "He's putting them near the embassy."

"Stupid idiot," mutters Kai. "What the hell is wrong with him?"

I flick off the computer. "When?" I ask as Esme starts to back away.

"I don't know."

"Maybe we can stop him!" My voice comes out like a breathy shout.

Kai turns away. "I'll call him, that's all. I'm not getting more involved than that. He's stupid and reckless and makes no sense."

"I'm doing my hair," says Esme. "And then I'm going out with Gash. None of this was my idea."

"You really won't help?" I look from Esme back to Kai. Kai's face is like a stone.

"No way," she says. "We could end up dead."

Esme seems stunned by Kai's last words. Her black mascaraed eyelids flutter up and down. "I do know when," she whispers. She's twirling a strand of long blond hair. "I mean, sort of—not *exactly* when."

I stare into her dumb, blank face. I can't believe she planned to keep this to herself.

"Sometime tonight. That's all I know."

LXXXI

I run home. I need to get some money. No one's there, thank God for that. I rush to my room, Smoky nipping at my feet. She knows that this is serious and it's almost like she's rushing me, urging me to hurry up. I grab my bag. Throw some dollars into it. I don't put on my ponytail. I can't believe I actually ever wore that thing. In the drawer with my socks, it looks like something dead.

The last thing I see as I leave the room is my mom's blue gown on the closet door. It stays for a moment behind my eyes, as vivid as a photograph. Tomorrow is her special night. Her life seems so sweet compared to mine.

I take a *remise* to Lucien's. *"Está esperándome"*—*He's waiting for me*—I say to the *portero*. He's the friendlier one and he lets me pass.

In the elevator I think of what I'll say to him. He'll probably be angry. He probably won't let me in. But maybe Solange will be at home. She'll usher me in and I'll tell her what Lucien plans to do. She'll be so grateful that I came, and later on Lucien will thank me too. Oh, God, I pray, let her be there. And don't let Lucien have left.

I shake that thought. He *can't* have left for Esme's yet. I don't think it's even seven o'clock. Yet when I reach the penthouse floor there's a quiet that feels like midnight. I can't explain it really. But the air feels hushed and still. I've been here a dozen times before, yet tonight it doesn't feel the same. It feels like a place I've never been. A silent, secret sort of place. I lift a finger to ring the bell and notice the door is not quite closed. I push it in, not breathing. And what I see behind the door sucks the air from a place so deep inside me, I never knew that place was there.

LXXXII

I run down the stairs, all fifteen flights, and through the lobby out to the street. On the street I run. I run like someone being chased. Past all the fancy, closed-up shops and the ivy-covered buildings onto the *avenida*, where the cars zip by like flicks of light. I run between the traffic. I run when the signal tells me STOP. I run and run until I can't. In front of the Alvear Palace Hotel, I stop and try to breathe, holding on to a lamppost in a pool of golden light.

The picture keeps flashing in front of my eyes. The instant when my father turns and the shirt falls open over his chest—the blue striped shirt that Nidia ironed yesterday, I saw her steaming the folded cuffs. His startled face. His wide, stunned eyes. And then Solange coming from the bedroom. In that silky ivory nightgown with the faintest trace of leaves.

The look on her face as it all computes and she whispers a faint "Ah, no!"

My throat constricts. There's a pain in my chest when I start to think of Lucien. Lucien knows. He knew and couldn't say the words. That was why he made me leave. I begin to walk. I don't know where I'm going. I move through fog, through murky air that quivers with sound and light. People pass but they don't have any faces; they're strange black shapes that float, slow motion, along the street.

I suddenly know where I have to go. I stop in my tracks and think of how to get there—of how to get to Noree's house. Noree will take me up to her room. She'll know what to say to calm me down. We'll sit on her bed with the daisy-patterned comforter, and that's what she'll do: She'll comfort me.

The lights of a car flash into my eyes, and I snap from my dream of Noree. Noree's not here and there's nowhere to go. Esme and Kai would probably laugh if I told them what was going on. My cell phone rings as if set off by the flash of lights from the passing cars. Like a robot, I take it from my bag. It's Dad. I think of what happened and where I am.

He must be frantic, the sick little worm. Crazed and frantic. Out of his mind. I stow the phone and walk again. I like to think how freaked and terrified he must be. Mr. Fidelity FBI. Mr. Tells-Everyone-What-to-Do. All freaked out. I can see him now. Pacing back and forth across the room. Sweating in his blue striped shirt.

The pleasure of that is like a whine that hums across my nerves. I put my phone on vibrate, and the satisfaction deepens every time I feel the pulse. I walk to the end of Alvear, past the bustling restaurants, the outdoor patios wound with light. I wander down the grassy slope and sink to the ground against a tree.

Thoughts of my mother come into my mind. Dad has probably called her, too, hoping to reach her first. He's made up some great big lie, of course. I'm sure he's said that I misinterpreted what I saw. He'll invent some reason for being there that she actually might believe. I think of calling her myself. I start to punch the numbers, but stop before I'm done. I could never tell my mother. I could never say the words to her. I picture her blue-green ball gown, hanging on my closet door, and a sob like a tsunami swells inside my chest.

I think of taking one of my pills. I think of taking *all* my pills and falling asleep in the cool, dark grass. But I don't even have the strength for that—the will inside to make a choice. I curl myself into a small, tight ball. The buzz of voices, the clatter from the restaurants, melts into a blur.

I can't have slept. But when I get up, I know that it's much later. The sounds from the places up the hill are echoey and softer now. There's a trail of music under the hum. The memory of what's happened snaps back into place with a sickening click. My cell phone jitters in my bag. There are twelve missed messages, all from Dad, each more desperate than the last. Then I catch the one from Kai. URGENT, it screams, and then the words:

THE AMERICAN EMBASSY NOT THE FRENCH.

THEY'LL SEND HIM TO GUANTANAMO!!!!!!!

LXXXIII

I'm running again. Down the hill to the busy web of streets below, bright with lights and traffic.

I stop for a moment to call a *remise*. Tell him where to pick me up. It's minutes to the embassy at the edge of the Palermo parks. In the back of the car I try to slow my breathing down. The statues in the park are white, luminous against the trees, like angels floating in the dark. I pound a one-word thanks to Kai. She has no respect for Lucien—nothing he does makes sense to her—but at least she told me where he is. She's right, of course; it's pointless, what he plans to do. It all has meaning in his head—*they lie to us, so I lie to them*—but no one really cares.

Solange and my father sure don't care. They only care about themselves. I can picture them now, pacing the apartment, dreaming up ways to cover their act. Plotting their excuses. They don't give a damn about Lucien. Why would they care what the boxes mean and what Lucien wants to say with them?

I get out of the car a block from the embassy. I can see the lights beaming in the guardhouse, and I realize anew how crazy and dangerous this is. It's an act of terror, my dad would say, even if the bombs are fake. Plus, no one will know the bombs are fake. They look so sinister and real. I wonder who's on duty tonight, if it's Carlos or Joe or one of the other marines I know.

When I'm closer I see the watchmen pacing the empty parking lot that runs along the gate. In the day-bright bath of streetlight I glimpse the gleam of buttons and the shine of their holstered guns. Kai doesn't live too far from here. Her parents are probably having dinner now; maybe they have guests tonight, Beatrice or Edda, and they're out on the rooftop, sipping wine. I weave my way through the quiet streets to the other flank of the embassy and the flat gray wall that faces Avenida del Libertador. There are trees and grass, and I know that I will find him here. That's where he will put the work, tangled in weeds, half-camouflaged to make it more mysterious.

I see a movement up ahead. It's low to the ground and I know that it is Lucien, running, crouching, placing the boxes along the wall. I make an arc as I approach. When I'm slightly ahead, I turn and start to come at him.

At first he doesn't see me. He's busy with his project. He seems to have a system; I think he's clumped the boxes, and he sprints back and forth to either side of the main supply. It's crazy that nobody has seen him. There must be cameras along the wall; even drivers passing on the road must see him in their beams of light. No; something isn't right. Something isn't making sense. And then it suddenly all comes clear. I picture them in the guardhouse, leaning close to watch him on the monitor, waiting to make their move.

He sees me at last. I whisper his name as he lifts his head. He freezes in place, a box in hand, his fingers on the long, dark fuse. For a moment I think the bomb is real. It *looks* so real and Lucien looks so wild, his cap pulled down, smudges of black smeared like war paint over his cheeks. He looks like a crazy martyr, like a suicidal bomber, everything hidden except his eyes.

"Lucien!" My voice shoots out across the dark. "They know you're here! We've got to go."

He stares at me, bewildered. "What are you doing? Why are you here?"

"Please just come! Just come with me!" I take a step forward. "You have to come!"

"Go away, Tess. It's dangerous."

"I know why you are doing this. Lucien—I *know*."

"What do you know?"

"I know—about *them*. I went to your apartment and both of them were there." A taste of acid burns my throat and floods into my mouth. Lucien's face is twisted. He looks grotesque, grimacing under the smears of paint.

"God," he groans. "I hate them. I hate them so much I don't know what to do with it."

"You knew and you didn't tell me."

"How could I tell you a thing like that?"

"I don't know." And I really don't. What I know is that we have to leave. I know that we are being watched. "Lucien, *please*,"

I whisper. For a drawn-out moment I'm sure I've failed—that he isn't going to come with me.

Then suddenly his shoulders slump. His entire body seems to lose its structure, and he stumbles across the space toward me. We start to walk very, very quickly, heading for the road. A voice calls out over the sounds of our rushing feet, over the hum of the passing cars.

"*Pare!*" it yells. "Stop! *Pare!*"

I know that voice. I'd know it anywhere—it's Jer—and it's coming from somewhere along the wall. Lucien and I do not *pare*. We do the total opposite and run like hell as fast as we can.

There's a sharp explosion in the air. It's a gunshot, but it makes no sense. Jerry can't *shoot* us, can he? It's hard to tell exactly where the shot came from, and it puts us in a panic and we flounder and run the other way.

There are more loud voices after that. "*Pare!*" they keep shouting, all of them. "*Pare! Pare!*" But how can we stop if they're shooting at us? We're near the end of embassy wall when three figures emerge from around the bend. They all have guns. Their arms are stretched in front of them, one beneath the other, supporting the small, dark weight.

"*Suban los brazos!*" one of them yells.

"Raise your arms!" That's Jerry's voice. I still don't know where he is.

"*Suban los brazos!*"

"*Pare!*"

"Stop!"

"Lucien, God, we have to stop!" I can hardly make my voice come out. It's like screaming in a nightmare, the sound like a whisper caught in my chest.

But we do. We *do*. We stop just like they tell us to. We halt in place and do not run. My eyes veer off to Lucien. Everything's in slow motion. I watch his hands—and I see that they're not going up. They're busy doing something else. There's a flicker of a yellow flame. The catching of the tail-like fuse. Then another awful burst of sound, and I fall to the ground as if I've been thrown by a gust of wind. An ocean of blackness closes in.

"Tessa. Tess." I hear my name whispered close against my ear, and it's like that day in the long red room.

We're on the soft alpaca, and his black kimono is slipping off. My fingers are running over the rune, the dark blue shape I scarcely feel on his cool, silk skin and it's silent and still, so silent, in the deepening afternoon.

Something disturbs the quiet. Loud, harsh voices yelling and breaking in on us. Then hovering and whispers. A voice I do not want to hear. "Girl's all right. But the boy's been hit."

That's all that I can tell you now.

THE
NEXT
PART

LXXXIV

Mom's fingers are white, gripped around the steering wheel. We've been driving for more than three hours now and she's hardly said a word. We're on our way to Carilo, the forested beach where all the city people go for family trips and holidays.

It's two days since the incident. We left Buenos Aires as soon as we could. As soon as I'd given statements and the police said we could go. Dad was there, but I wouldn't even look at him. He and Mom talked in private, and when we got home, she told us to pack.

"It's lucky there were rooms," she'd said as she raced around grabbing clothes for Tyler, stuffing every suitcase full.

"Where are we going?" Tyler had asked, watching Mom fold his winter coat.

"Take everything," she whispered in the hall to me. I stood there and stared.

"I can't," I said.

"You have to."

"But Lucien—"

"Tessa, I know. But there's nothing you can do for him."

"I can't leave Buenos Aires now. I don't even know if he's—"

"We'll make phone calls, Tess. We'll keep checking in."

"But he's—"

"I need for you to be with me. I need you like I've never needed you before. Now pack your things. Anything that matters. Anything you think you'll need."

"Nothing matters."

"Tessa, please."

"Where is Dad?"

"Go pack your things."

I hardly take anything at all.

So here we are, escaping to the ocean as if we're the ones who made the world go upside down. I'm in the front with Mom, and Tyler's in back with Smoky and whatever bags wouldn't fit in the trunk.

Mom's told him some crazy story. She couldn't possibly tell the truth. Dad, she said, was going to join us later; right now he was on a "special case."

"Is it dangerous?" Tyler wanted to know, and Mom said something funny: "Dad knows how to take care of himself."

The scenery is monotonous. It looks like the pampas to either side, endless fields of beach grass swaying in the sun. I keep checking my phone. I haven't heard from anyone. I don't expect Solange to call, but Esme and Kai must know by now. How could they not call me—if only to say hello? The softness of the landscape—the billowing grass, the cotton clouds—rubs all wrong against my nerves.

LXXXV

There is sand on the road long before we actually get to Carilo. The grass to either side of us is now replaced by pine trees, delicate and sparse. There are taller trees as we travel on, and before too long the road is hemmed with huge gray trunks that bloom high up in the mild blue sky. Mom's grip on the wheel loosens a bit. I think the pine trees soothe her. They're so sheltering and still.

We drive past the tiny central town with its small boutiques and artisans' booths. We pass chalets and cool, half-hidden weekend homes. It's almost Christmas, so lots of families are already here. I watch them through the window and they seem like rare, enchanted beings. Moms and dads in their casual vacation clothes. Kids with their dogs, gathering pinecones from the ground. Pinecones as big as loaves of bread.

We drive to the very edge of the sea. It's the end of the earth and that's why Mom has chosen it.

The hotel is pretty fancy. We have a suite with a wall of glass that faces the sea. It must be quite expensive, but Mom, I guess, doesn't care right now. Plus we need the space because Bill is coming to join us here. Dad apparently called him first, and Bill called Mom, who told him where we'd be. Dad, of course, has ways of finding out himself, but I don't think he'll try to follow us here.

As soon as we settle into our room, Tyler wants to go to the beach. So that's what we do. We walk through the marble lobby, out the back, and down a windy dune. The sand is brown, not white like the sand we're used to, which makes it look wet and cold.

Actually, it is quite cold. The wind is strong and carries needles of chilly spray. Mom was right to make us take a sweater. Along the beach, clumps of people lounge on blankets and canvas chairs, talking and laughing, bundled up in the breezy sun. I feel as if we have nothing to do with any of that. With happiness and normalcy. Even Tyler and Smoky look strange to me, running along the water's edge, totally oblivious. Mom looks like a mannequin. As if she's afraid to move her face. As if every breath is like a stab.

LXXXVI

Mom makes a reservation at the fancy restaurant downstairs, but in the end none of us wants to go. We really do try. We put on some decent-looking clothes and go down to the buzzing lobby. But the hum of voices floating from the open doors, the echo of a sparkly piano, send us back upstairs. We order room service and put on our pajamas. Tyler's thrilled; it's what he wanted from the start. He snuggles up with Smoky and they eat their hamburgers on the couch.

I go out to the terrace and sit with Mom. She's drinking wine and her face and jaw are softer now; she seems to be drawing normal breaths. She pours me a glass as if to say she's always known, and I wonder if she has. We pick at the food—a plate of shrimp and vegetables—and stare out at the sea.

"I should have told you a lot of things." I suddenly hear my own low voice. "I think if I'd told you certain things—"

Mom keeps looking straight ahead. "How could you tell me anything if I wasn't there to hear?"

"You were there. One day I went to talk to you. I knew, I

was sure, you'd understand. I was going to tell you everything. About Lucien and all my lies. And how Jer was following us around."

"I know when that was. Your father was there. We were sitting around the swimming pool."

"How did you know?"

"I felt it, Tess. Just as you felt I'd understand." Mom shakes her head. "But Jim was there, and he hadn't been there—with me, I mean. I was so afraid—and so I let the moment pass."

"You knew about—?" I watch her as she shuts her eyes. She keeps them closed when she speaks again.

"I didn't know who. And I had no proof. It was just a feeling I had inside."

Her eyelids twitch and she shakes herself. "I can't talk about your father, Tess. I can only talk about you and me. And I let you down in a terrible way."

"You didn't," I say. "I waited too long to talk to you. And by then I was living some other life. You have no idea the kind of stuff we were doing, Mom." She tells me again that it wasn't my fault. That the problem was with herself and Dad. That if they'd been intact—if their unit had had integrity ("the *I* in FBI," she says)—I would have been able to trust in them and things would have turned out differently.

"It wasn't your fault either!" I'm almost yelling through my tears. "It was Dad who—" But that's where she cuts me off again.

"I told you, Tess, I can't discuss your father. There were things I didn't want to see. I knew they were there—or sensed them—but chose to look the other way. I got all caught up in changing myself instead of facing what was really happening." She wants to own all the blame herself, but it doesn't all belong to her. I wake in the night and think of all the things I did. I think of things I didn't even want to do. How I did them just for Lucien. I loved him more than I loved myself. And like my mom, I saw only what I wanted to see. I knew that he was losing it. I felt him falling away from me and I couldn't let go, so I followed him there. Right to the very edge.

The suite is huge and we make Mom take the bedroom. Tyler and I each have enormous pull-out beds. I'm sitting on mine when Mom walks through. The cell phone's glowing in my hand. At last there's a text from Kai. Lucien had surgery, he's still alive; that's all we know. Mom comes over and looks at it.

"I'll call tomorrow, Tess," she says.

"Will you?"

"Yes. I'll find out everything I can." She kisses my head. "Now say a prayer and go to sleep."

Once she's gone, I move from my couch and curl up next to Tyler. I wrap my arms around him, thinking he is Lucien. He's Lucien and Tyler and Mom and Bill and everyone I've ever loved. *Please, please God, don't let him die. Make him survive and be all right.*

LXXXVII

A whole day passes between the time Mom gets the news about Lucien and Bill arrives at Carilo. If there hadn't been that space of day, that dreamlike interval of time, I couldn't have gone to meet the bus in Pinamar. I couldn't have watched Bill climbing out, looking so like Dad in his polo shirt and khaki pants, with his dark and ruddy tan.

But there'd been the day. The long and separating day when all I did was cry.

LXXXVIII

Bill comes to the beach to find me. I've been sitting here since I left them in the restaurant. I couldn't even have tried to eat. I know it's him by his heavy footsteps in the sand. He sits down next to me and wraps a second sweater over the one that's not much use.

"Mom said you'd need it," he murmurs then, like he doesn't want the credit for a thought that wasn't his.

"Thanks," I say. I wrap it around me like a shawl. "How'd you escape from Tyler?"

"Mom helped with that. Plus I think he's tired." We sit for a while not talking, listening to the crashing waves. Then he lets out a breath and turns to me. "I need to know what happened, Tess."

"Mom told me that you talked to Dad—"

"Don't call him Dad—"

"What am I supposed to say?"

"I don't know. Let's call him Jim. No, better yet, let's call him Jimbo from here on in."

"Jimbo?"

"Yeah. Just call him that." Bill nods his head, like it makes the name official. "Anyway, Jimbo didn't tell me shit. He just told me about his 'big mistake.' Fuck," he snaps, and smacks a fist against the sand. "He screwed around with your boyfriend's mom! What the hell is wrong with them?"

"Solange didn't know he was my—" I cut myself off before the "dad."

"I don't understand how she wouldn't know."

"They move in different circles, Bill. Dad's a nobody next to her."

"But *he* sure knew, now didn't he?" And when I don't say anything: "Listen, Tess, I know it's hard. But you have to explain some things to me. I obviously can't talk to Mom." I shift around in the little nest of sand I've made. "I just don't get it, Tessa. Did Mom not really have a clue?"

"Come on. Be fair. It's easy to see when we look back now, but at the time we thought he was traveling for work. He certainly let us think he was."

"What a bastard."

"Yeah, I know. But think of it, Bill; he'd been away for two whole years. He and Mom were out of touch. Sometimes I think that Dad felt sort of obsolete."

"Don't make excuses for him, Tess. He was probably always screwing around. Even down in Bogotá."

"I'm the last one who'd make excuses, Bill. I'm just trying to understand. One thing I know—it's hard to keep things going when someone isn't there." Bill doesn't answer, and I go on. "Now that we know—it's funny—it almost seems so obvious. When Solange was in town, so was Dad. Same thing with the traveling. I'm pretty sure it first happened in Paraguay."

"*So-laaaange,*" says Bill, dragging out the syllables. "What kind of name is that—*Sol-aaaange?*"

She's really nice, I almost say. I think of the night at *La Bohème*. My heart still winces, remembering how we drank champagne and she talked to me about Lucien as if I were her friend. But Bill would freak if he ever knew I liked her, if he ever knew how beautiful I thought she was. He'd disown me if he knew the truth: that I understood how Dad could fall in love with her.

Sometimes I imagined it. Solange and Dad passing in an airport. Their flight's delayed, so they linger in a quiet bar. Maybe Mom was mad when he left that day. Solange is soft, a little tired from traveling. Maybe to her, Dad looks strong and craggy, not weak like Lucien's fancy dad. They start to talk, and it just sort of happens by itself.

Bill would never understand. He's older than me, but he doesn't know about stuff like that. How things unfold and happen right in front of your blinded eyes.

"Tell me about that night," he says. His voice has an almost tender tone. "What was Lucien trying to do?"

"Guerilla art," I answer. I could almost laugh at how stupid it sounds. "He made these boxes designed to look like IEDs. He'd found out about Solange and Dad. It was all about deception. Dad was such a hypocrite."

WHEN YOU OPEN YOUR EYES

"Yeah, for sure. But what Lucien did is crazy, Tess."

"I know it is. That's why I went to stop him. He was already laying the boxes out. I knew they had to be watching him. And I was right. Jerry was managing everything."

"Jerry? *Jer?*" Bill looks at me like I've lost my mind.

"He was stalking us for months. He said he had to—that it was his job."

"What is that supposed to mean?"

"He said that he 'takes care of folks.' If he sees someone in danger, he has to intervene. It wasn't just me; he watched all the American embassy kids."

"So he followed Lucien that night? Did he think the boxes were actual bombs?"

"I have no idea what Jerry thought."

"Because if he did, he should have let other people know."

"Jerry was Napoleon." Lucien's words come out of my mouth, and something cracks at the top of my voice.

"I'm sorry, Tess," Bill murmurs. "But I have to know what happened to our family." He waits awhile, motionless beside me. He isn't going anywhere, and I know I might as well tell him now. If I look at the sea—if I focus on the bright, uneven hem of white that ripples the edge of every wave—maybe I can say the words without falling apart and flying back to that place I can't ever go again.

"I'd persuaded Lucien to leave. We were already getting out of there when Jerry starts yelling for us to stop. We're panicked, you know, so we both just ran. Then crazy Jerry fires a shot—"

Bill's face is pale, incredulous.

"He shot in the air, I later found out."

"He's never heard of *gravity*?"

I don't even answer. I just go on. I'm afraid if I stop, I might not make it to the end. "The guards come running the other way. They tell us to stop and put up our arms. Lucien was terrified. He wanted to scare them away from us, so he struck a match and put it to the so-called 'fuse,' so they'd think the bomb was real—" I suddenly can't continue. There's a knot in my throat like a bone-dry rag.

"So Jerry shoots him?"

"No." The word ekes out from behind the knot.

"What then, Tess? What happened?"

There's a raspy pain as I force my voice. "It was one of the marines. You remember Carlos, right? Carlos shot at Lucien."

"Ah, hell," says Bill. "Oh, Tessa, hell." He nudges sideways in the sand and wraps me in his arms. In the back of my mind I wonder—who is going to hug old Bill when it all sinks in and he realizes what this means for him?

LXXXIX

Bill says what everyone will say. That it's lucky Lucien didn't die. I say to him that tragedy is funny. Different people handle it in different ways. Mom found out that Lucien's father hurried in from Paris. He and Solange are going to bring him back to France, and they're going to live together again. It's over for me and Lucien. After this, what could I ever say to him? It's not just about our parents. How could I forgive him for what he let happen to himself?

He didn't die, but the bullet bore into his spinal cord, and he's paralyzed below the waist. Yes, they'll say, he's lucky; at least he'll be able to do his art. But he'll never ever make love again the way he did with me. Never again for all his life.

XC

The four of us walk into town. It's sunny and warm and the air is spiked with pine and salt. The rustling of the treetops is as steady and reassuring as the sound of the ocean waves at night. We walk around and look at the booths of handicrafts. Tyler buys Smoky a woven gaucho-style leash. Mom buys me a really pretty scarf and a cotton sweater the color of sand. We stop to eat at an outdoor place. There are giant pinecones all around, and Tyler collects the biggest ones and throws them around for Smoky to fetch. It's almost like we're normal, and for long, sweet minutes at a time I forget what's actually going on and lose myself in the simple pleasures of the day.

Then back at the hotel, everything explodes. Dad calls Mom. Of course, we knew he eventually would, but I wish he could have waited and let us have this interlude—this tiny, quiet moment in the forest by the sea.

Mom goes into the bedroom and closes the door behind her, but we hear her voice, quiet at first, then loud and shrill, to the point where she's hysterical, screaming through her tears. I've never heard my mom like that, and it scares me half to death.

Then something crazy happens to Bill. I see the flicker in his face, a twitch of the jaw that makes him look so much like Dad. He bolts from the chair and tears into the bedroom.

After that, all hell breaks loose. I hear Mom crying really loud and screaming incoherent stuff. Then I hear Bill. He's yelling at Dad on the telephone, calling him a piece of shit and other words I didn't even know he knew. I can't believe these people are my family—my pretty mom, my straight-as-an-arrow father, and my sweet and simple brother Bill—all screaming and yelling and out of control.

And then I remember Tyler. I spin around and find him in a corner, huddled against the wall. Tears are running down his face and Smoky is trying to lick them off. I grab his arm and pull him from the hotel room.

Out in the hall we can still hear Mom, her high-pitched wail like the sound of an animal in pain. I drag Tyler outside and down the dune to the windy beach, where the sound of the surf washes the echoes from my ears.

I hold his hand and we run and run, Smoky at our heels. We run near the shore where the waves come in, and when we're exhausted and can't go on, we stop and topple onto the sand and I hold him in my arms. I tell him about a million times that everything will be all right. That in the end we'll all be fine. I tell him I'll take care of him, and this time I will, I really will.

XCI

om stays in her room all evening. She tells us through
the half cracked door to go somewhere for dinner,
but none of us wants to leave her alone. Plus, who's
in the mood to eat? All the same, Bill orders some food—french
fries and pizza, stuff like that. He tries to get Mom to take a
plate, but she won't open the door to him.

She's been talking and talking on the phone. We can hear
the murmur of her voice but we can't make out the words. I
hope she's talking to a friend, yet I bet it isn't Sandy Blaine or
Anne McDermott with her seven perfect kids. I kind of suspect
that her embassy friends are as useless as my own new friends,
who seem to have forgotten they ever knew my name. I've
texted Kai and Esme a dozen times throughout the day, and
neither has answered back. My one true friend is Lucien. And
Lucien is gone.

At midnight or so, Mom emerges from the room. She's pale
and looks exhausted. Her eyelids are red; the color almost looks

painted on. Her gaze moves slowly around the room and settles on the three of us. We're all in a clump on a pulled-out couch, Smoky curled on Tyler's lap.

"Want some food?" Bill asks at once. "There's leftover—"

"I don't want anything," she says. "I just want to say that we're going home."

A flood of pictures sweeps into my head. I suddenly see my bedroom—the *Water Lilies* blues and greens, the shadowy closet where I hide, and the window filled with light. And I want to go home so much it hurts.

But that's not what Mom means by "home."

XCII

I can't believe we actually have a Christmas tree. It looks pathetic standing in the corner decked with plastic ornaments. But it would have been impossible to open the box Dad shipped from Argentina (a desperate and pathetic plea) and find the ones we've always hung. The crystal balls, our names and birthdays scrawled in silver glitter ink, the clothespin reindeer, Play-Doh stars. There might as well be a skull and crossbones on the lid.

The tree's for Tyler, according to Mom. I can't imagine what he thinks. One day he has a family and the next day he has nothing. Does he care about a Christmas tree?

So here we are. Mom makes breakfast and serves it in the old, familiar dining room. It's pretty late, like eleven o'clock, when Bill comes down in his wrinkled sweats, shuffling in his Guatemalan espadrilles. It's all he ever wears these days.

"Hey, Bill!" says Tyler, pulling out a chair for him. Smoky Girl is happy too, wagging her tail and running around. Tyler's put a big red ribbon around her neck. I wish to God he'd take if off; the sight of it makes me want to cry.

"Did you sleep well?" asks Mom coming from the kitchen. Already her highlights have dimmed a bit. She's made pancakes, bacon, and little rolls. I'm glad she remembers how to cook.

"Like a baby," says Bill, plunking down in the chair. He's lost a fair amount of weight, and is more messed up than anyone. It kind of makes sense, since he'd always modeled himself on Dad. He wanted to *turn into* Dad. And now he has to start from scratch and find a new person to become.

We sit around the table. We look like those people you see on TV who've just survived an earthquake. The ones who look like zombies as they search through the wreckage of their homes. Mom serves the food and tries to act like we're okay. There's a tablecloth—not the one from Paraguay—and a centerpiece of evergreen. The sun slants in through the old sheer curtains she's hung on the windows facing the yard.

"Aunt Jean has asked us for Christmas Day," she says as we begin to eat.

"Great," says Bill. "I'll only go to your side now." I never even thought of that—what happens to the relatives—Dad's sister, Kate, and my grandparents, whom I really like. It just gets bigger every day. I never knew how one small thing, one single choice, can devastate a world. I wish that Lucien had known.

I don't know what else we talk about. Just small talk, I guess. How Mom has to do some shopping. How she needs to buy more kitchen stuff. Bill wants to know if I've seen Norah. I haven't. Not yet. If I saw her face I'd fall apart; I'm too tired to fall apart again. It's dull and kind of comforting to sit and talk about stupid things. Yet it isn't as easy as you'd think. So many things have tangents that go back to our life and the way it was, which always included Dad.

XCIII

Bill knocks on the door. Comes into my room. He's still wearing his crummy sweatpants and hasn't combed his hair.

"Hey," he says. "Can I sit down?"

"You can try, I guess." I think of the last time he came to visit me in my room. My beautiful *Water Lilies* room. He sat on my plushy armchair, and toyed with a pillow in his lap. The long, tall windows were full of branches and twinkling light.

My bedroom here is piled up with cartons, which Mom got Dad to ship express. I just can't seem to open them yet. There are FRAGIL warnings all over them, though they're only filled with clothes. It seems like the perfect label for everything in our life. He finds a sturdy-looking box and plants himself on top.

"Do you believe this shit?" he asks. He lets out a breath and looks around. I shake my head. For a minute he just stares at me. Then he says in a quiet, almost gentle voice, "I've decided not to go back to school."

"Don't talk like that."

"I'm serious. Everything is different now, and I've got to decide what I want to do."

"You already know what you want to do."

"Oh, yeah? What's that?"

"You want to finish college, go to law school, and join the FBI."

Bill lets loose with a big fake laugh. "Like hell I do. That's the last thing I want to do with my life." He shakes his head. "I've got to think of something else. I'll take a couple of courses here. Mom, I'm sure, would like it if I stuck around."

I don't want to break the news to him, but what Mom wants most is for Bill to take off and get back on track. She keeps asking about his courses, if he's worked out a schedule and stuff like that. She wants him to get out of here and stop moping around in those smelly Guatemalan shoes. And as much as I love him, so do I.

"Listen, Bill, you've always been clear about what you want. And unlike me, you've always been sure about who you are. Remember in Buenos Aires—you told me how much I'd changed. I told you that I hadn't—that *that* was the person I'd always been and that Mom and Dad were holding me back. It wasn't true. I wanted to be *those* people, the people I was hanging with. I wanted to live their fast, free lives—no parents, no rules, the whole world at their fingertips. But you can't live someone else's life." I stop for a moment; I'm saying things I hadn't put into words before, and it makes me slow down and listen to my own strained voice. "It's the same for you. You aren't Dad, no matter how much you tried to be. The life you live can only be your own." I'm talking to Bill, but I'm talking to myself, as well. Maybe I'm talking to all of us.

XCIV

Christmas comes and then it goes. I'm glad when it's all over. It's hard to be with people. Others, I mean, who aren't us.

One night I think of Esme. She's in Venice now. I imagine her in her Russian hat and Solange's tall black boots. I picture her in a gondola with Gash and old Evangeline; it's dark and they're drinking cold champagne, and I can't for my life believe I ever knew them. They've disappeared, and I never hear from anyone. Esme. Kai. Not anyone. There might have been Paul if I'd let him in. But I never did, so he's gone too. The past is unreal, and everybody in it seems like a character from a dream.

School is going to start next week. I'm dreading it like you can't believe. I tried to get Mom to let me take the semester off, but of course she told me no. It's the only way I'll ever get back to normal, she says. She seems to think that such a thing is possible. But how can I feel normal when the center of my life is gone? It matters to her, I don't know why, that I graduate with my class. I'll be glad, she keeps saying, a year from now.

I can't imagine a year from now. Or two years, or five. I almost can't bear to think about years because when I do, I always think of Lucien. Years from now—ten or even twenty years—he'll still be in a wheelchair, and that will always be his life. How do I get past this truth?

XCV

Noree comes over one afternoon. I told her not to; I feel ashamed to see her, knowing now what a really lousy friend I've been—no different than Kai and Esme were to me. But she doesn't listen and comes to see me anyway.

She's standing in the kitchen—Mom let her in—and the minute I see her Noree face, I forget whatever I said to her and run into her arms. We go to my room and climb onto my bed like it's a boat. She cries when she hears about Lucien.

Bill comes by while we're sitting there. He hasn't seen Norah in ages now, and the two of them have a big reunion in my room.

"You really look great," he tells her. And it's true, she does. She was always pretty, with huge brown eyes and dark brown hair, but she wears a little makeup now and she's let her hair grow long. I think it has to do with Mike.

Bill thinks the same and says so. "It's love," he teases. Then: "How's old Mike?" Noree blushes and looks at me.

"Yeah," I say, "how is he? All of us want to know." It's all right with me to talk about Mike. I'm happy for them now. And it seems like a million years ago that I thought I was in love with him.

"Did you tell her what happened?" Bill asks next.

Noree nods. "I'm really sorry . . . about your dad."

"He's not my dad."

"Oh, yeah," I explain to Noree. "Jimbo's his name, from here on in." It seems funny now, and I almost laugh. So does Noree— sort of—and even Bill cracks half a smile. It feels so strange to almost laugh. Like the surface of my skin might split. That's how long it's been for me.

"Sit down," says Noree, making some space on the bed for Bill. So the clod climbs in beside her. We can hardly fit—my stupid brother takes too much room—but the three of us squeeze in anyway.

"So what about Jimbo?" Noree asks. "Is he going to come back?"

"He better not," my brother says.

"He's still in Buenos Aires, then?"

"Yeah," I say. "It's funny. Nothing happened to him at all. As far as anyone's concerned, the shooting had nothing to do with him. He was miles away. Did not even know what was going on."

"I bet his assistant got the ax for shooting in the air like that."

"Nah," says Bill to Noree. "The FBI never fires assholes. They just reassign them to New York."

"Then it's Carlos who probably got the ax. The regular guy just doing his job."

"Yeah," says Bill. "And isn't it ironical that all that time while Jer was keeping tabs on Tess, Dad was having a big affair right under his dumb-ass nose." We sit for a while, not talking; then Norah says, "I can't believe you didn't want to come back to school. What were you planning to do all day?"

"Nothing," I say. "Just hang around."

"You can't do nothing all day long."

"I actually can. I've gotten really good at it."

Bill agrees. Like he should talk. "It's like a form of art for her. Which, by the way, Tessa's given up. Art, I mean. She says it's over: She's lost the ability to draw."

"You'll get it back," says Noree. "You just need a little time." She grabs my hand and says in an energetic voice, "I have lots of plans for us, you know."

"Oh, really?"

"Yeah. I hated when you went away. I tried to be okay with it, but it really wrecked my life. Now that you're back, I plan to make up for the time we lost. I missed you so much, you can't believe."

"Shit," says Bill. "I'm going to cry."

"Shut up," says Noree, punching him. She turns to me. "Listen, Tess, it's horrible what happened—but you still have good things in your life. You still have me. And you have your great big brother here. I never knew what a sensitive guy he actually is. You have your mom. And you still have Tyler—he's so sweet—I wish I had one of him at home."

"Maybe we can rent him out." Bill's trying to be funny

because way deep down he's really touched that Noree called him sensitive.

"You're the world's best friend," I say to her. "But I just can't imagine being in school—with the way I feel and with everyone knowing what's going on."

"Nobody knows what happened. And I'm not telling anyone. As far as your parents are concerned, nobody cares about stuff like that. Lots of parents are divorced. It happens every day."

"I never thought it would happen to us."

"Yeah, I know. But life is weird. School will keep you busy. Kind of take your mind off things. Plus there's stuff coming up—stuff that's fun. And you and I—well, we get to get hang around again."

"Yeah, Mike will really go for that."

"Is that what you're afraid of—that Mike is somehow mad at you?" Noree grins. "Well, he isn't, you know. He was hurt at first, when you broke it off, but I managed to get him past the pain. Mike's very happy now."

I think of how I never wrote back when she told me she was seeing him. And that makes me think of another *what if*: What if I'd kept in touch with her? What if she'd known what was going on? She would have been smart and clear-eyed. She would have given me good advice, and maybe . . .

The therapist I'm seeing told me to make a "what if?" list. She thought it would make me realize that most of what happened wasn't my fault. But my list makes me feel the opposite.

I get to the twentieth *what if*: What if I'd told my mother that Lucien was ill? And it always comes back to me.

"Mike's lucky," I say to Noree, changing the subject in my head. "I'd much rather be with you than me." We hang around for a while more, and then she has to go. On the first day of school, she promises, she and Mike are going to come and pick me up. He got a new car. Well, not really new, but new for him.

Another *what if* comes into my head. What if we'd never gone away? What if I were still the person I was before—that girl with Mike, that sort-of happy person, who walked around with her eyes half-closed through every minute of the day?

But what's the point of wondering. I can't go back. And would I want to if I could?

XCVI

It's hard for us when Bill takes off, though I'm really glad he does. He said I was right—that he can't give up his goals and dreams just because "Jimbo fucked things up." That's how he put it. Bill's own words.

Before he left he did a brave thing. He called Buenos Aires to talk to Dad. He told Dad what he thought of him—how once he wanted to be like him, but now he just wants to be himself. He told Dad he thought he was phony. That Dad didn't know what Fidelity meant. Or Bravery or Integrity. Bill let Dad know that even if he never joined the Bureau, he'd live by the values they espouse, and be a better man than him. I don't know how he did it. I know I couldn't talk to Dad.

I never felt proud of Bill before. I mean, really proud, like yay, hooray, that's my brother, everyone! I knew that what he'd said was true. And I knew that Bill was really strong and from here on in would always be taking care of us. It makes me feel safe to think of that. I haven't felt safe in a really long time.

I miss him a lot in the first few days. Now it's just the three of us: Tyler, Mom, and me. And Smoky, of course, who probably wonders what happened too. Tyler talks to her a lot. I hear him in his bedroom, chatting away as if she's Sam McDermott or one of his friends from down the street. I'm glad that he talks to Smoky, but I'm also glad that he talks to me.

Every day we walk the dog together. There's a wooded park right near our house, and we wander through the winding trails. It's cold, but kind of beautiful. There's some leftover snow in places, and the ground has an icy sheen of dew. We usually go about four o'clock. It's just at that point before the sun starts going down. In a little while, the sky gets streaked with color—orange and purple and reddish pink—etched with the silhouette of trees.

XCVII

It's the end of February now. Noree's all excited about the big St. Patrick's Day dance in March. She's head of the planning committee and is handing out jobs to everyone. She left me alone for Valentine's Day, but now she's back, full force.

"Tessa," she says in the car one day. "You're in charge of decorations. You're the only one with any artistic talent. And you can't say no—you owe me big."

Mike agrees. "You owe her, Tess. She's been taking very good care of you."

I can't believe they still keep picking me up each day. It's a good thing they do. Mom's back at school, so I'd probably oversleep a lot. She never finished her master's degree on account of Bill's coming into the world, and now she's decided to wrap things up. She wants to teach high school, who knows why.

As for Mike, things are fine. It was awkward at first. That very first day when they picked me up. Mostly I felt guilty. And a little embarrassed, because he has someone and I'm alone. And I'm the one who threw him off. But the truth of it is that he and

Noree are really good together. Better than I ever was with him.

It's a bleak afternoon. The sky's sort of white, like it's going to snow. Tyler's friend Tommy is here today, and they're watching a movie in that place we call the family room. The name seems really stupid now.

Anyway, I'm thinking of decorations. Shamrocks, of course. And leprechauns. Those silly golden harps. I start to think about Celtic stuff—the Byzantine plaits and knots and swirls. I remember that I have a book. I have lots of beautiful books on art.

Upstairs in my room, I dismantle a pile of cartons. Underneath I find the box, the one I've tried to keep from sight. ART SUPPLIES/BOOKS it says on top. Dad must have hired some English-speaking person to label the boxes as Nidia packed. I stare at it for half an hour. It makes me think of Pandora's box and all the demons trapped inside. I almost do not open it. I push it aside and throw some pajamas over the top. But I know it's there, and sooner or later I'm going to have get to it.

The first thing I find are brushes and paint, and under that, my pencils. I take it all out and lay the items on my bed. I'm slow at coming back to the box. I drag another carton close. I have to sit down to take a breath. In the first of the sketchbooks I find the watercolor scene—the Japanese bridge and the tree-lined pond. I taste the day on the tip of my tongue—petals and grass, a hint of water in the air. I find some drawings I did at school— the view of the river from under our tree, sailboats tilting in the wind. I come to a sketch of the mausoleum, the swirled design of its ironwork door. It's like an ache, remembering.

I find a bunch of circles. Chiquita banana. A button. A screw. I picture them lying on various floors—on bathroom tiles, on kitchen slats, in the dark of the Marine House under the couch where we sipped the gin. The wandering halls. The closet underneath the stairs. The first time ever in my life.

Loose pages fall. There's the drawing of my Nazi dad that Lucien did that afternoon when Esme took his mother's shoes. And here's the sketch of my big rose dress. He drew it as I walked around. My beautiful dress. My huge dark rose. It slipped like water under his touch. And oh, his touch. His mouth along my collarbone, in the heartbeat of my throat. I find the picture of Lucien. The one of his face that I did in school. I almost can't bear to look at it. It gives me an actual physical pain in a spot between my ribs. But I force myself to do it—to look into the dark, still eyes I know I'll never see again.

He's the one I loved first. And he loved me, too. *I won't ever forget you, Lucien, even when I'm old and gray—an old, old girl in a red wool cap.*

XCVIII

I make giant golden Celtic knots. Celtic-style dragons. Peacocks, snakes, and mermaids, and wild-looking fish. I make crosses and circles and letters wound around themselves eating their own swirled tails. Doing my little project makes me remember working at the Casa. In the box I find my beaded dragonfly and pin it to my shirt. At least I know there was one good thing I did in Buenos Aires.

As I paint my gold medallions, I wonder if I could do that here—find someplace to volunteer. Some hospital or something. For kids who are sick or people like—people hurt, like Lucien. The thought grows brighter in my head. I can't stop thinking as I paint. And I can't stop painting as I think.

Noree's thrilled with my designs, and her team of workers loves them too. They make me help them decorate. I go to the gym and we hang the huge medallions. We tape them to the bleachers and tie them on strings from the metal beams. It seems like I've made a million, and we plaster them over every wall. We strew the place with streamers and set the tables with bright green paper cloths.

I guess I'm going to a dance. I don't remember what that's like. I think of the stuff I did for fun back in Buenos Aires. I was usually high, and the places were dark and it always felt slightly dangerous. Maybe a dance will be all right, sort of soothing in a way. Scratchy music. Soda. Chaperones at tables trying to look invisible.

Mike and Noree drive me home in the drizzly falling dusk.

Dancing feels really strange at first. And then it feels sort of comfortable. I'm a butterfly sprung from a tight cocoon. If I tip back my head and swirl around, the light makes me think of sunshine, falling through star-shaped leaves. Golden shields are hanging from the ceiling. Long green streamers graze my hair.

When I focus my eyes, Jason Greer is jumping around in front of me. He's swinging his arms and his wild red hair is flying out. He smiles when he meets my eyes, and I start to jump up and down like him. I'm sure I look ridiculous. Yet it doesn't feel ridiculous. Instead it feels like something everyone should do. I mean, if you can—if you can move your arms and legs, you ought to be jumping up and down.

I know this tonight as I twirl around in the patchy light. How close I came. How lucky I am. The beat of a heart, the blink of an eye. Within a *hairsbreadth*, as they say.

My legs are loose and free and strong. The music is loud and pounding. I'm doing a wild ritual dance—a dance around a fire or a dance in the pouring rain. Even Jason looks rare and beautiful. His goofball grin could take your breath.

C

There's another thing I have to do. I've bought a special pencil case. And a canvas bag for my pad and paints. I've constructed a mat so that I can sit on the cold, damp ground.

CI

Mom's at school and Tyler's off with a friend today, so I go to the park alone. I bring my insulated mat and my little bag of art supplies. I walk through the trees. Through the beaten paths the people have made on their weekend walks. But it isn't the weekend, and no one is here. The sun is sinking toward the west, and the air has a winter evening chill that creeps inside my coat. There's a silence like a sleeping breath.

The lingering ice crunches softly under my boots. I find a place near a clump of fallen branches, and set my mat on the crisp, brown leaves. I open my bag and take out my pad and the tray of paints. That's when I see it—the bright green sprout, piercing the earth like the tip of a knife. There are others nearby, a field of them, poking through the icy leaves.

I don't know why it startles me. Why the freshness and greenness is such a jolt. I must have thought the world would stop. That everything was over and nothing would ever grow again. But that's not how it is. It all goes on. Hours and seasons and time and life. Even now, the day gives way to sunset—the dark pink fire, the purple edge. There isn't a moment left to waste.

I soak the page with my widest brush, laying the paint in a long, broad stroke. The trees are black on the burning sky, and everything looks so pure and clear.

ACKNOWLEDGMENTS

Deepest thanks to my serene and ever-supportive agent, Erica Rand Silverman.

Thanks also to Annette Pollert for meticulous editing, for gorgeous hand printing, and for helping the chapters bloom.

Finally, a kiss to friend-readers Mary Antonelli, Maureen Knapp, and Stanley Hoffman. You're in my heart.

ABOUT THE AUTHOR

Celeste Conway is a writer and artist. She currently resides in New York City.